Rafe's eyes were closed, his chin tipped up, as he stretched the kinks from his muscles....

My, how she'd love to run her fingers down the naked length of him. She could only imagine how hard, how sculpted, his body would feel.

Libby tightened her grip on the chopsticks until she feared they'd snap in half.

Soft blue denim hugged his butt. And what a nice, tight butt it was, too.

Libby grinned. She was being so bad. She knew it, and it was so unlike her. But what harm was there in checking out the view? she wondered, her smile widening.

What she'd really like was to see his slick, black river of hair flowing free against the bare flesh covering the wide, strong expanse of his muscular back. To feel those silken tresses against her own naked flesh. A loose and languid chuckle rose in her throat, and she did her best to stifle it.

"What has you grinning from ear to ear?" he asked.

THE COLTONS

Meet the Coltons—
a California dynasty with a legacy
of privilege and power.

Libby Corbett: *High-powered attorney.* She came home to clear her father's name. But now that her life is in jeopardy, this take-charge woman must entrust everything to one man—a man who has a chip on his shoulder almost as big as her own!

Rafe James: *Native American rancher.* A proud loner, he knows the only way to help the town through its crisis is to get close to the *one woman* who threatens to topple all his defenses.

Blake Fallon: *Tough-to-tame director.* In spite of his rules against mixing business with pleasure, anyone can see there's something going on between the Hopechest Ranch's director and his loyal assistant....

Todd Lamb: *Ruthless tycoon.* Now that he's been named head of Springer, Inc., all the long hours he's spent devoted to his work are about to pay off. Or are they?

CLOSE PROXIMITY

Donna Clayton

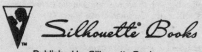

Published by Silhouette Books

America's Publisher of Contemporary Romance

Special thanks and acknowledgment are given
to Donna Clayton for her contribution
to THE COLTONS series.

 SILHOUETTE BOOKS

ISBN 0-373-21750-1

CLOSE PROXIMITY

Visit Silhouette Books at www.eHarlequin.com

Printed in U.S.A.

ABOUT THE AUTHOR

DONNA CLAYTON

is fascinated with Native American cultures. After
researching the traditions and philosophies of various
Pacific Coast Indians, she strove to create what she
hopes is a richly textured history and a strong present-
day sense of community for the fictional Mokee-
kittuun tribe featured in her story. An award-winning,
bestselling author, Donna lives in Delaware with her
husband and Jake, their six-year-old Border collie.

This book is joyously dedicated to fellow authors Maggie Price, Jean Brashear and Cara Colter. Ladies, you made this a rollicking adventure, and I'm grateful to the bones to have had this chance to work **with** you.

One

The steps of the courthouse were crowded with camera-wielding media, placard-waving radicals and other individuals who were just plain curious. And to think, Prosperino used to be such a sleepy little town.

With traffic at a standstill, Rafe James sat in his pickup truck watching the circus unfold before him. The irate anti-oil-company chants of several ringleaders could be heard even though his windows were rolled up tight against the chilly March morning.

Having lived most of his life on the Crooked Arrow Reservation, Rafe didn't travel into town often anymore. Nearly everything he needed could be bought or bartered for right on the reservation, so Rafe didn't have much to do with the outside world these days. There simply wasn't much need, unless he had a side job going.

Two different insurance companies called upon him at times to do a little investigative work. And he also used

Prosperino as a base for meeting with buyers for his beloved horses. Equestrians from all over the world had purchased the Appaloosas he bred and trained. He didn't think of this as a bragging right, just fact. A fact he took pride in.

For the most part, Rafe kept to the rez, among his own kind. However, he'd found himself drawn into town every single day since David Corbett, the vice-president of Springer, Inc. had been arrested. The need for information regarding the oil company's problems had Rafe's investigative antennae on alert, urging him to listen to gossip, devour each newspaper article he found on the case, study every word of the local evening news. Hell, the story had hit the national news lately. And it was going worldwide, he realized when he saw the CNN van parked up the street.

No way was David Corbett guilty of the disregard for human life and attempted murder charges he was currently facing. The man was too honest, too fair-minded, too compassionate, too honorable to have intentionally tainted the water supply with DMBE, or any other chemical, for that matter. Rafe didn't care what the EPA had discovered, or that the evidence shed a poor light on Springer's ex-VP. And Rafe wanted to laugh when he'd read the FBI's so-called theory.

Oh, someone *had* deliberately contaminated the water. And that someone was involved with Springer. But the Hopechest Ranch for children hadn't been the target as the FBI believed. And neither had the town of Prosperino.

Rafe had his own suspicions about this whole mess. But who was going to listen to an Indian playing a guessing game filled with speculation and conjecture? Nobody, that's who.

All Rafe knew for sure was that David Corbett was innocent. Rafe's gut told him the man was being used as a scapegoat. And if there was one thing he hated, it was when someone took the blame for an offense he didn't commit, when someone was forced into the role of victim.

Victim. The very word turned Rafe's blood to acid. Memories swam and churned in his head. But he cut them off, strangled the life out of them before they had a chance to come into focus.

This wasn't about him. It was about Corbett.

Rafe sighed as he thought about the dire straits the man was in. But Rafe knew him to be intelligent and savvy. Surely, Corbett would get himself out of this tight spot. He'd find himself a good lawyer. Surely, the evidence could somehow be refuted—

Like the eyes of an eagle homing on prey, his gaze zeroed in on the woman who exited the front doors of the courthouse. The morning sun glinted off the long tumble of her hair, turning it the color of polished copper. Immediately, she was besieged by media people hounding her with questions. The radicals pressed in on her as well, shouting slurs, chanting angry accusations.

Her chin was tipped up defiantly as she faced down what she so obviously saw as the opposition. Confidence seemed to ooze from her, and the tiny hairs on the base of Rafe's neck stood on end. Something deep in him stirred—

A horn blared behind him, and instinct alone kept him from starting. He couldn't believe he'd become so wrapped up in the scene on the courthouse steps, or in the red-haired beauty standing there.

Darting a glance in his rearview mirror, Rafe saw the irate motorist mouthing and gesturing an obscenity. Reacting to such nonsense never even entered Rafe's head. Instead, he searched for and found a parking spot, pulled in his truck and cut the engine. He was out on the sidewalk and making his way toward the courthouse before he even had time to think.

This morning he hadn't intended on doing anything more than picking up the daily paper, but instinct had changed his plan. He was being urged into action by the overwhelming need to discover who the woman was. If the Elders had taught him anything, it was to listen to his gut. One's very life could depend on heeding what might seem to others as sheer impulse.

What an odd thought. But he didn't take time to reflect on it. By the time he reached the base of the brick steps, the mob was descending toward him and the woman was pushing her way through the crowd.

"David Corbett is innocent," she told them all. "That fact will be proven.

Strong vehemence girded her statement, and Rafe got a shadowy sense that those words—that tone—just might put her in peril.

"I'll stake my entire career on it. I have nothing further to say at this time."

The media continued to pepper the woman with questions, but she remained stonily silent as she moved through them, doing her best to brush aside the microphones being shoved at her.

"How can Corbett ever refute the mountain of evidence against him?"

Her skin, Rafe noticed, was like creamy porcelain.

"Wouldn't it be easier for everyone if Corbett simply pleaded guilty to all charges?"

She moved with grace and style. The woman was poised. Even under fire.

"How does he feel about Springer turning its back on him?"

Her fingers were tapered, her nails neatly manicured with clear gloss. The thought of them raking down the length of his chest burst into his mind, unbidden, and Rafe's jaw clenched in reaction.

"Have you taken a leave of absence from your law firm in San Francisco? Or are you taking this case with your boss's blessings?"

Her eyes were an astonishing aquamarine. Clear. Earnest. Intelligent. Connecting with them for the first time was enough to make a man feel as if he'd been kicked in the chest by a wild stallion.

"What did David Corbett say when he learned that his job was taken over by Todd Lamb?"

That gaze of hers brought the ocean to mind. The wide-open Pacific on a bright, still afternoon. A man could get lost in those eyes.

"As Corbett's daughter, do you really feel you can set aside emotion and successfully represent your father in this case?"

This final query caused the woman to blanch. She blinked, her well-shaped mouth parting just enough for her to inhale a quick breath. The confidence expressed on her delicate features slipped a notch. As hard as she tried to hide her reaction behind a reflexive swallow and a small plastic smile, the sudden vulnerability clouding her blue-green gaze affected Rafe.

Mightily.

Reveling in her utter beauty hadn't been his only pursuit of the last few seconds; he'd also absorbed the reporters' questions and all the information the nonstop grilling had suggested. He knew who the woman was, where she was from and why she'd arrived in Prosperino.

Shouldering his way into the crowd, he stepped between the woman and the last television correspondent who had spoken.

"Back off." The tight expression Rafe offered the man and the threat lacing the edges of his tone had the reporter retreating automatically.

Lightly grasping the woman's elbow, Rafe focused every nuance of his attention on her. There were questions in her eyes. He saw them. But now was not the time for answers.

"Where's your car?" His voice was quiet. Meant only for her.

She pointed, and he led the way. Miraculously, the horde parted and allowed them access to the sidewalk and the cars that were parked along the curb. He opened the driver's door and she slid behind the wheel, thrusting her attaché case onto the passenger seat beside her. The engine sparked to life, and after offering him one quick look of gratitude, she pulled into traffic and drove off down the street.

Libby Corbett pulled into the driveway of her childhood home. She sat in the quiet, her hands resting lightly on the steering wheel as she stared at the huge white Victorian house with its fancy gingerbread trim. As a little girl, she'd spent many an evening curled up on that porch swing between her mom and dad. They had been an incredibly close-knit family of three; racing and cavorting in the shade of the trees out in the backyard in the spring, playing board games at the kitchen table on rainy winter evenings, making up songs at the old grand piano in the living room, reading the classics together in her parents' massive king-size bed.

She'd been in junior high school when she slowly became cognizant of all that her parents had sacrificed in order to accommodate her special needs, in order to keep her feeling safe and secure. The opportunities to travel they had given up. The social life they had let pass them by. All for her sake. They had understood how uncomfortable their daughter had felt around people.

The severe stuttering problem that had plagued her all through her adolescence had made her painfully shy. She'd grown up virtually friendless. It was nearly impossible to make friends when you refused to speak.

However, her parents had succeeded in filling in all the gaps in Libby's life, and her memories of growing up in Prosperino were filled with happiness and joy. Through her high-school years she'd worked hard to overcome her speech impediment. She'd so wanted to liberate her parents of the worry they suffered on her account. She'd been desperate to somehow free them, to give them back their lives so they could enjoy each other and the world around them. But just when intensive speech therapy seemed to have put that goal within her reach, fate had dropped yet another obstacle into the path of the Corbett family.

When her mother had been diagnosed with breast cancer, Libby knew it was her turn to become the caretaker. And she had done everything she could to make her mother's load lighter. She'd rushed home from school to cook and clean. She'd done the shopping, the laundry. She'd accompanied her father to the hospital on daily visits. She'd knelt by the toilet, holding a cool, damp cloth to her mother's forehead when the chemo treatments caused such violent vomiting. When her mom's silken hair had fallen out in clumps, Libby had refused to cry, choosing instead to run out and buy several colorful turbans she knew would bring a smile to her mother's wan and weary face.

Libby had done everything in her power to be strong for her mom, to somehow pay her back for all the love and caring the woman had showered on her.

Sandra's cancer had gone into remission, but the disease had taken its toll on her emotional welfare. The years of battling had stolen her zest for living. And then in '97, the cancer had returned.

Both Libby and her father had nearly died of grief when Sandra Corbett had passed away. Their terrible loss had only made them closer. When it came time for her to start her career, Libby had balked at leaving her dad all alone, but he'd gently pushed her out of the nest so that she could test her wings. With a law degree under her belt and her exciting job with a prestigious firm in San Francisco, Libby was terribly grateful that her father had allowed her the freedom to fly. There simply wasn't enough room in the entire universe to contain the love Libby felt for her father.

David Corbett had been her champion when she'd been a little girl. Her knight in shining armor. He'd sacrificed so much for her, made her feel secure, made her feel loved at a time when the awful stammer she suffered made her feel flawed and awkward and often stupid.

Years ago, Libby had been strong for her mother through those long months of her illness. It had about killed her to keep her chin up and a smile on her face, but she'd been proud to offer a shoulder for her mom to lean on. Now the time had arrived for her to be strong for her father. Now was her opportunity to repay him for his years of total devotion and sacrifice.

When her father had called her to request that she find him a good lawyer, Libby hadn't a clue why he might need representation. She'd assured him that she could take care of any personal legal matters he might have. She might be a criminal attorney, she remembered telling him, but someone in her firm could certainly see that his will was properly filed.

Her knees had grown wobbly when he'd finally confessed that he was calling her from jail and that he was facing felony charges.

Disregard for human life? Attempted murder?

That very evening the story had hit the west coast newspapers.

How could anyone—the EPA, the FBI and least of all the executives at Springer, Inc.—believe that straitlaced David Corbett could be guilty of those crimes?

Libby had immediately gone to the partners in the firm and requested time away from the practice in order to give her father the best representation available. No one had a greater stake in this than she did. No other attorney would be willing to go to any lengths to prove her father's innocence like she would. Together, she and her father would beat this thing.

Uncertainty, gray and thick, gathered around her like a wintry coastal mist.

Why had her father balked initially when she'd proposed she travel north to act as his lawyer? She hadn't really thought about it at the time, so caught up was she in his plight. Why had he tried so hard to decline her offer of help? Sure, he'd used the excuse of not wanting her life interrupted by what was sure to be a mess—the biggest three-ring circus in the history of Prosperino, he'd said. He'd tried to reason that her professional reputation might be in jeopardy just by having her name associated with the case. However, she couldn't help but wonder if, just maybe, her father doubted her ability as an attorney.

Maybe he thought she didn't have the skills necessary to successfully clear his name.

"But I can help you, Daddy," she whispered in the solitude of the car, wretched emotion burning her throat, unshed tears prickling the backs of her eyelids.

Fear gripped her belly with icy fingers when she thought of all the hostility she'd faced at the courthouse today. From the media. From the townspeople. Everyone seemed so dead-set against her dad. Everyone.

Suddenly she remembered the rich, mahogany eyes of the man who had come to her aid this morning. Never in her life had she experienced an expression filled with such complex and concentrated intensity. The memory made her shiver.

When the man had touched her, when he'd taken her by the arm, the chaos in her mind calmed. She'd felt safe. Secure. He'd been like a harbor in the midst of a terrible storm.

But that was silly. Safe and secure with a complete stranger? Come on, Libby, her brain lectured. You're letting down your guard.

That protected feeling had simply come from the fact that he seemed to be on her side when no one else had been. The man must know her father, must have had some dealings with him. The thought brought her comfort.

Maybe everyone wasn't against her father.

She inhaled deeply and tipped up her chin. She sure wouldn't be able to clear her father's name by wallowing in doubt and self-pity.

The car key was cool against her palm as she pulled it from the ignition. Shoving open the door, she exited the car, bringing with her the bag of groceries she'd purchased this afternoon and her attaché case. With a small thrust of her hip, she closed the car door. The heels of her shoes clicked on the paved drive as she made her way to the porch.

Libby looked up and was truly astonished to see him standing on the front lawn. The man with those intense, dark eyes.

Two

He was a big man. Tall. Lean. Powerful. And his features looked as if they'd been chiseled from some golden-hued stone from the desert, his cheekbones high and sharp, his jaw angular.

Without conscious thought, her steps slowed, then stopped altogether.

Something about his stance gave the impression that he was primed, ready. To attack or flee, she couldn't tell which.

Just then the afternoon breeze tangled itself in his long, raven hair, whipping it across his eyes and jaw, obscuring his face from view. An odd, out-of-the-blue urge welled up in Libby, and she had to fight the impulse to go to him, to brush back his hair, experience what she easily imagined would be the silken texture of it between her fingers. The startling thought made her eyes go wide, made her heart trip in her chest.

In the calm of the moment, she realized he was the most luscious man she'd ever laid eyes on.

That astonishing notion made her suck in a quick breath. What on earth had gotten into her?

She suppressed a smile when she realized that just because experience had forced her to swear off men entirely, she was still a woman. The feminine part of her demanded its right to appreciate a good-looking man when she saw one.

With an economy of movement, he turned his head, lifting his chin a fraction, and the wind whisked his hair back over his shoulders. And massive shoulders they were, too. Her eyes slid down the length of him. Over his broad chest covered by a white button-down shirt, narrow hips belted with a strip of suede decorated in a beaded, distinctly Native American design. His jeans, denim worn soft and supple with age, encased muscular thighs.

A desolate sigh whispered across her brain as she imagined him naked. The thought nearly made her choke.

She forced her gaze to the sculpted features of his face.

Who was he? And what was he doing here?

As much as she wanted to focus on the issues important to the here and now, she couldn't stop the unbidden perceptions from flashing in her mind like sharp bolts of lightning.

Untamed. Stealthy. Panther-like.

Each description that zipped through her thoughts caused a friction that heated her blood.

He didn't seem in any way unrefined or brutish. But... feral. Yes. That was it. A wildness exuded from him like heat radiating from the sun. Natural. Genuine.

Libby realized her heart was hammering and her mouth had gone as dry as the California desert. Enough of this, she silently ordered. When her feet still didn't move and her tongue remained cleaved to the roof of her mouth, she silently ordered, Enough.

Suddenly she was moving again, and rather than making her way to the front door as she'd first intended, she veered toward the man.

"I didn't get the chance to thank you this morning," she called to him. "For helping me escape those reporters at the courthouse."

Until now his countenance had expressed a tentativeness as if he wasn't quite sure he should approach. But now his tense features relaxed, if only a bit.

"I'm Libby Corbett. David Corbett's daughter." As soon as the introduction left her mouth, she silently decided he must realize those facts already. How else would he have known where to find her?

His steely silence made her nervous. "Can I help you with something?" she asked.

"I was thinking that maybe I could help you."

She remembered the commanding tone he'd used when addressing the reporter this morning. But now his voice sounded rich. Resonant. And a delicious tremor coursed down the full length of her spine.

"Oh?"

It was the only answer she could pull from the fog of her thoughts.

His mouth and jaw line went taut, and Libby got the distinct feeling that he'd somehow gotten his pride knocked out of joint, that maybe her one, tiny response had somehow belittled him. Although his boots remained planted in the grass, he turned his head, obviously considering making an exit then and there. She could tell.

"Wait," she called. She took several steps toward him, leaving the concrete, her high heels a hindrance in the thick grass. The bag of groceries grew heavy suddenly and she shifted them into her other arm. "You know my dad?"

His nod was almost imperceptible.

"You know something about the case? You can help my father?"

"I'd like to help him."

The fact that he hadn't answered the first question wasn't lost on her, but she offered him a smile anyway. She felt as though she'd sailed into a sea of enemies since arriving in Prosperino. Anyone who was willing to help her dad would be considered a friend until she had some reason to think otherwise.

"Would you come in for a cup of coffee, Mr....?"

"James. Rafe James."

"Well, Mr. James—"

"Rafe."

"Well, Rafe. You'll have to call me Libby, then, won't you?"

The smile he offered her was small, but it provoked an amazing response in her. Thoughts turned chaotic as images materialized in her brain. Sensual visions of that wide mouth of his raining kisses over her body.

It had been so easy to conceive of this man as wild, animalistic. But now it was just as easy to picture him in the role of tender lover. In any other puzzle, those two opposing pieces wouldn't go together. But with Rafe James, they somehow fit.

Perfectly.

What a ridiculous notion. This man was a complete stranger to her.

Shoving the inappropriate thoughts from her mind, she said, "So, should we go in?"

He nodded slightly and then moved toward her.

The muscles of his thighs played under the fabric of his jeans, and Libby had to force her eyes to avert to the ground. Before she realized it, he was close. Very close. He smelled like citrusy cedar and leather, and she had to force herself not to close her eyes and get lost in the scent.

"Let me take this for you."

When he reached to take the bag from her, his hand brushed her upper arm. The desire to protect herself by stepping away from him was great, as was the urge to move toward him, ever closer.

She did neither, and she thanked her lucky stars that she had sense enough to keep a level head on her shoulders. She had no idea what had gotten into her. The stress of worrying about her father's tremendous troubles, she guessed. That and the despair of having gotten caught in the memories of her childhood.

After unlocking the door, she made her way through the house to the kitchen, very aware that Rafe James was close on her heels. She set her briefcase on the ceramic tile countertop of the island.

"Set the bag here," she told him. Then she silently indicated that Rafe should take a seat on one of the high stools.

"So, how do you know my dad?" Libby busied herself putting away the quart of milk, the loaf of bread and the other groceries she'd purchased.

He didn't answer right away, and his apparent hesitancy made her pause. With a bag of apples still in her hand, she lifted her gaze to his.

Finally, he said, "I don't want to give you the wrong impression. David Corbett and I are not and have never been friends."

Libby's brows drew together, but she remained silent, waiting.

"Sixteen years ago," he continued, "your father hired me at Springer. I'm—"

The rest of his thought was cut short and he pressed his lips together. He took a moment to inhale, and Libby's gaze unwittingly darted due south as his chest expanded. She blinked, and immediately directed her eyes to his.

"Let's just say I'm grateful to him."

He went quiet. Once she realized he didn't mean to say more, she pulled open the refrigerator, placed the apples in the bin, then shut the door, pausing there with her hand on the stainless steel handle.

"You went to the trouble to search me out," she said, "and offer my dad your help during this crisis, all because he gave you a job sixteen years ago?" She raised her brows. "Must have been one hell of a job."

Moving across the room, she reached for the coffeepot and began filling it with water.

The sigh Rafe emitted sounded resigned. "He made me a security guard. Gave me a fair wage. A job with health benefits. Saw to it that I received thorough training. And I was able to use that training for more lucrative employment after I left Springer."

As he talked, she placed a paper filter into the basket of the coffeemaker and spooned in the ground beans. Something about Rafe James's motives just didn't ring true. His manner was...reserved. Cautious. And had been since he'd first appeared out on the front yard. She poured the water into the reservoir and snapped on the machine.

Libby had been hurt by one secretive man in her past.

She wasn't about to fall prey to another—in any aspect of her life.

Whirling around to face him, she blurted, "So let me get this straight. You went to the trouble to search me out, and you want to help my dad, all because he gave you a job and properly trained you for that job." She shrugged. "Seems to me my dad was only fulfilling his responsibilities."

Her short, sharp laugh didn't hold much humor, but conveyed instead a huge measure of skepticism. "My father has worked for Springer for nearly thirty years. I'm sure he's hired lots of people. My front door is going to fall off its hinges if every single one of those grateful people come racing to help."

A thunderous storm gathered in his mahogany eyes. She hadn't meant to make him angry, but she felt it necessary to be blunt about his flimsy reasoning. Almost of their own volition, her arms crossed tightly over her body.

He stood, and the sheer size of him coupled with his surly expression was a daunting sight, to say the least. A person with any sense at all would feel afraid. However, she didn't, and that wasn't because her brain cells had suddenly gone dim, but because, although muscles bunched in his shoulders and ire sparked in his dark eyes, she knew in her heart she was perfectly safe with this man.

"Look, Ms. Corbett, you're right when you said your father has hired lots of people over the years. And many of them are just like me."

The emphasis he placed on those last three words made her frown.

Just like him? He was Native American. Most probably from the Mokee-kittuun tribe living on the Crooked

Arrow Reservation just outside of town. But what did his ethnic group have to do with this? Although the question disturbed her, the confusion she felt kept her silent.

"For years," he continued, "the people from the rez weren't given a second glance when they applied for work at Springer. Your father did everything he could to change that. And as he moved up the corporate ladder, he continued in his efforts. Continued to treat us with fairness and respect."

As she listened, her shoulders tensed until tiny needles of pain began shooting up her neck. In all the years that her father had worked at Springer, he'd never once intimated that there was any kind of racial discrimination at the company. Yet here this man was, telling her that her dad had spent his entire career battling what sounded like an anti-Native American sentiment at Springer, Inc.

"He's even helping our children," he said, intense emotion tightening his facial features. "The first thing he did when he became Springer's vice-president was to set up a scholarship fund for reservation children. And when he visited the Elders just before last Christmas, seeking to lease some of our land so that Springer could expand, did he become angry when his request was turned down? No. Instead, he was moved by the living conditions of the people. His heart was touched, and he offered to have Springer cover the cost of a new well—a well that was being dug up until the moment he lost his job."

She wished an abyss would open up in the floor and swallow her whole.

Anger now ticked the muscle of his jaw. "Where I come from, a man who gives respect earns respect. It's something that's not given easily and not taken lightly. Your father is a good man. He doesn't deserve the treatment he's receiving. He's completely innocent. And I think he could use a friend, Ms. Corbett."

It was hard to meet his gaze, but she forced herself to do it. She moistened her lips. What could she say to him? Coming from the reservation, having been born into an ethnic minority, he'd probably seen more than his fair share of bigotry and narrow-mindedness. An apology, she silently surmised, would seem almost offensive at this moment.

Feeling the need to make some sort of response, she offered him a small and sincere smile and let her arms relax at her sides. "I thought you'd agreed to call me Libby," she said, keeping her tone friendly.

The turbulence in his gaze settled somewhat, but his emotions continued to brew, that much was easily discernible.

She tried again. "Please sit down, Rafe. Let me get you that cup of coffee."

He was measuring her, the situation, the moment. She couldn't tell what all was going through his mind. But it was obvious that her attempt at a pleasant tone, a laid-back demeanor, was beginning to soothe his ruffled emotions.

Libby had never met a man quite like Rafe James. He seemed so vigilant, watchful, as though he wasn't quite sure from where trouble might come at him. It wasn't that he seemed paranoid, really. Just…ready for anything, she supposed.

His manner could stem from his very existence. Hadn't he just explained that he'd experienced more than his fair share of prejudice?

Or it could have roots in his very makeup. In his genetic material. Native Americans had a rich history filled with an ancestry of hunters and brave fighters. Could the

DNA of the wary and wild warrior be carried down through the generations?

Realizing that she'd allowed herself to get carried away with fanciful notions, which was quite out of the norm for her, Libby straightened her spine and sighed.

"Rafe, sit. Let's talk."

His whole body seemed to relax finally, and he did as she bade.

The smell of coffee was heady as she brought the cups to the island. She set one down in front of him, then retrieved the sugar bowl, creamer and two spoons. It didn't surprise her to see that Rafe took his coffee black. She slid out a stool and perched herself on it right next to him.

"So...you live at Crooked Arrow?" she asked. It wasn't an outrageous guess. He'd insinuated as much.

Rafe nodded, his long, ebony hair falling over his shoulder.

The urge to reach out and comb her fingers though the shiny mass of it made her tighten her grip on the cup she held in her hand.

"I have a horse ranch. Breed Appaloosas."

One corner of his wide, full mouth curled upward, and Libby found her gaze drawn to the spot as if it were a powerful magnet.

"Every nickel I could spare while working at Springer was put aside for the ranch. It was always my dream. And now I'm living it."

For an instant, the muscles of his face eased...and Libby's breath caught in her throat. He was truly a gorgeous man.

At that moment, he smiled, open and easy, for the very first time, and it seemed to her that all the oxygen had been sucked right out of the air.

"Now that you've discovered that I deal in horse-flesh," he said, "I guess you're wondering how I could possibly help your father."

In all honesty, Libby quietly responded, "I hadn't, actually." Then she added, "But I'm sure you'll tell me."

"Because of my extensive training all those years ago at Springer," he told her, "I was able to qualify for a P.I. license. I've worked for a couple different insurance firms in the area. You'll be needing someone with my skills, I'm sure."

Coming from anyone else, that statement might have sounded cocky, overly prideful. But Libby didn't feel that way about it at all. She admired the fact that he was confident.

She didn't answer, but simply lifted her cup to her lips and took a sip of coffee. For some reason, she wasn't ready to come to any kind of arrangement with this man.

Softly, he said, "Your father is lucky that you're a lawyer. No one would fight harder for him than family."

She actually flinched when she heard him mirror the very thoughts that had passed through her mind earlier when she'd been sitting out in front of the house in the car. Luckily, coffee didn't slosh over the rim of the cup.

"You practice in San Francisco?"

"Yes." Her tone made it clear that she was surprised by his knowledge of her.

"You've been mentioned in the papers," he explained. "And there's been plenty of talk about your arrival. Prosperino is a small town. Rich soil for the old grapevine."

She only nodded. The sound of his voice had a lulling, mesmerizing quality.

"You look like him."

Libby's gaze darted to where the pad of his thumb absently traced the gentle curve of the lip of his cup, and she was bombarded with a vision of that thumb roving over the outline of her mouth. Her throat went dry and her eyes darted from his.

"Your father, I mean," he continued. "You inherited his hair coloring. Although, if I remember correctly, his is a much darker red. But your eyes…they're quite different from what I remember your father having. His are dark, aren't they?"

She nodded. "I've got my mother's eyes."

"I see."

It seemed to her that he wanted to stop there. She could see his silent, internal battle. A battle he ultimately lost.

"Your eyes are quite—" His rich tone lowered an octave as he added, "Startling."

Libby swallowed, her spine straightening.

Startling. It was a word Stephen had often used when describing her gaze. And it was a description she'd come to loathe.

This conversation was getting much too personal for her tastes. The porcelain cup clinked firmly against the tiled countertop when she set it down. "So…what makes you think my father is innocent?"

He was very good at masking his reactions, but Libby did see his dark brows raise a fraction in surprise before he reined in his response.

"I've already explained. Your father is a good man. His heart—his conscience—would not allow him to poison the land. Or the people living on it."

"Good people do bad things every single day," she pointed out.

"I may not know him personally, but David Corbett has a strong sense of right and wrong. He's shown that over and over again to my people."

His gaze shifted, and she got the distinct impression that he wasn't telling all he knew.

"Let's just say," he went on, "that my gut tells me he is innocent."

Caution seemed to pulse from him. And he said no more.

Memories of Stephen flooded her mind, bringing with them a wave of pain and emotional agony that became nearly more than she could bear. Before the thoughts and feelings could get a foothold, though, she shoved them away from her, far to the back of her brain.

She didn't need another secretive man in her life. Personal or professional.

Libby had been hurt in the past by a man who refused to reveal all, and she was determined not to be duped by another. But then the scene on the courthouse steps came rushing vividly into her mind. So many people seemed against her father. So many people wanted his head on a platter. And Springer and the authorities seemed happy to supply the length of her dad's neck for the offering. The case seemed mountainous. And she felt terribly alone.

Maybe, she thought, an uneasy alliance with Rafe James was better than no alliance at all.

She tipped up her chin, her decision made. "Okay," she said, reaching her hand out to him, "so we're in this together."

Without hesitation, he slid his hand in hers.

Three

"**I** can't believe the judge denied bail."

Rafe remained quiet as he watched Libby pace the length of the room. She was livid. And seeing her caught up in all that fury, he was struck by the sheer glory of her.

"A flight risk? How could they believe my father would run? Everyone in this town knows him. Well, most everyone, anyway."

Turning around, she strode back toward him, her gaze dipping and roving wildly, seeing nothing, as thoughts so obviously careered through her head at lightning speed.

"He'd never run. Never. His only intention is to clear his good name."

Her aquamarine eyes blazed with heated emotion, her long auburn curls bounced with the anger fairly pulsing from her waving arms and jutting shoulders. She was surely a sight to behold.

Finally, he felt compelled to quietly ask, "Did you know he'd planned the trip?"

He remembered how shocked she'd looked when the D.A. had requested that bail be denied due to the risk of David's fleeing the country.

"*He* didn't plan the trip," she told him. "*I* did. Before Christmas. He loves to ski and the skiing in Canada is great this time of year."

Her gaze latched on to Rafe's, and the shadows that clouded her eyes tore at the very heart of him. She was feeling guilty. That much was plain.

"I've been begging him for years to do something fun. I pushed extra hard this year. I even booked the flight and hotel myself. I wanted him to get away and have a good time. Even if I had to bully him into doing it." She sighed. "I fully expected him to cancel the reservations. But he didn't." Softly, she added, "And I remember how happy I was about that."

The deep crease etching her brow marred her beautiful face.

"This was going to be the first trip he'd taken…"

A lump of emotion seemed to swell in her throat. She attempted to swallow around it, and the effort seemed painful.

"…since Mom died." Her gaze glittered with moisture. "Rafe, they've confiscated his passport, the airline tickets, everything. They really do believe Dad's a flight risk. They really believe he's guilty of these charges."

So, the reality of things was setting in, Rafe saw.

Yes, she was an attorney. In her San Francisco practice, she represented myriad clients who faced allegations just like these every single day. Rafe was sure she had understood the seriousness of her father's predicament all along; however, when it came to one's family, it was hard for a person to really imagine anything bad happening. But it seemed that the direness of her father's situation was finally sinking into her head…into her heart.

The sympathy Rafe felt ached from down deep in his soul. He didn't want to care about this woman. Couldn't afford to. Caring made a man weak. And he'd vowed years ago, that weak was the one thing he wouldn't allow himself to be.

But seeing her haunted gaze, understanding the frustration she was experiencing, imagining the guilt she was feeling over what she saw as her part in providing evidence against her father in the form of those trip reservations, Rafe couldn't just sit by, see the misery in her gorgeous eyes and do nothing. But he didn't dare surrender to his desire to touch her. He didn't dare yield to the urge to take her in his arms and reassure her.

Instead, he said, "Did you ever think that maybe David is better off behind bars?"

She whirled on him. "How can you say that? That place is horrible. He's penned up in that little cell with nothing to occupy his mind. He's—"

"Got three hot meals a day," he interjected, "a clean, warm bed to sleep in and a bevy of armed guards to protect him."

That's more than you have at the moment, he wanted to remind her. But he didn't.

Bewilderment wrinkled her forehead.

From the moment he'd spied her on those courthouse steps, heard her declaring loud and long her intentions of clearing David's name, Rafe had experienced the strangest sense that Libby might be in danger. Not from the reporters and not from the picketers. But from someone. Some unseen, unknown force.

When he'd sought her out at her father's house to offer

his investigative services, something gut-deep made him hold his tongue regarding his opinion that she needed a bodyguard. Working for her as a P.I., he'd figured, would give him plenty of opportunity to keep a watchful eye on her. And after having spent some time getting to know her, even if it had been just a couple of days, he knew for certain that she wouldn't appreciate hearing that he thought she was in any kind of jeopardy. She was most definitely the kind of woman who felt certain she could look after herself. Maybe, though, he could plant a small seed of warning in her head by using her father as an example.

"Someone dumped that dimethyl-butyl ether," he quietly explained. "And since we both know David wouldn't go near DMBE, then the guilty party is out there somewhere. Waiting to see how things pan out. Hoping your dad takes the fall."

Her brow smoothed somewhat. But then her brilliant, jewel-toned eyes glittered with new understanding.

"If there is evidence that points to David," Rafe continued, "then it just might be unwise for him to be walking the streets, if you know what I mean."

She nodded, silent and suddenly pensive.

He didn't want to frighten her. Fear often paralyzed rather than readied a person. His only intention was to make her aware of reality.

"Speaking of evidence…" He'd made his point, he felt, so now was the time to change the subject. "What's the D.A. got on David that would lead to this arrest? Can they actually prove anything?"

"Well, I can't say for certain until I get my hands on copies of the evidence. I've filed for discovery. Soon we'll have access to everything: physical evidence, depositions, police reports...'' She shook her head. ''It must be a mountain of stuff.''

He shot her an expression that had her expounding on her last statement.

''The day I arrived in Prosperino,'' she said, ''the police searched the house.''

''You allowed that?''

She shrugged. ''They had a warrant. But I wouldn't have stopped them. Dad said he had nothing to hide. That he gave his permission for the authorities to search anything and everything he owned.'' Libby sighed. ''They carried out a whole file cabinet and boxes of other files as well. Everything that had anything to do with his finances—bank records, credit card statements. And his PC.'' Again she shook her head and shrugged. ''A mountain of stuff. And there's no telling what was seized from his office at Springer.''

''It can't all be evidence against him.''

''No.'' Reaching up, she absently combed her fingers through her thick tresses. ''I don't expect anything from home to point to Dad's guilt. But I am worried about his office at work. Anyone could have had access to it since his arrest, couldn't they? And the prosecutor will use the other things—the information about Dad's finances—to try to explain motive, I'm sure.''

Silence settled over them, and while Libby busied herself with thoughts of her father's case, Rafe took a moment to look around him.

The Corbett home was huge compared to houses on the rez. The floors were constructed of rich, golden-hued oak, waxed and gleaming, and covering them were Oriental carpets that were most obviously costly. The room was elaborately trimmed in decorative moldings at the baseboard and around the ceiling. Such detail spoke of money. The furniture was heavy, luxurious stuff. Many pieces looked, to his untrained eye, to be antique.

He imagined Libby growing up here. Running and squealing and laughing through these rooms with caring parents to tend her, nurture her, love her. He pictured Libby enjoying holidays eating at the long, walnut table he'd seen in the dining room. Blowing out candles on a fancy birthday cake. Decorating a Christmas tree here in the living room. Celebrating Independence Day with sparklers and cookouts in the spacious and shady backyard.

A youngster would have enjoyed an idyllic childhood in this lovely house. A pampered and pleasant existence surrounded with lots of family and friends.

Visions of his own youth came flooding into his mind, and seemingly out of nowhere hot emotion prickled the backs of his eyelids.

What the hell? he wondered. Shoving against the arms of the chair in which he sat, he stood and paced to the nearest window. Not because he wanted to see the view, but because he needed a moment to collect himself, to force these damned thoughts from his mind. He hadn't allowed memories of his past to affect him like this in years.

It was Libby. She was making him care. She was making him soft.

He couldn't afford that. He couldn't.

"We're arguing trial location tomorrow."

Rafe nodded, but didn't turn around. He was glad for something to focus his attention on. "Trial location?" he asked.

"Opposing counsel wants to go to Los Angeles," she said. "He's looking to make this high-profile. But I want to stay here. I know there are lots of people ranting against the contamination. Against Dad. But I'm hoping things will calm down and they'll remember who's on trial here.''

She'd be safely cloistered in the courthouse during the day, he thought.

''And what would you like for me to do while you're occupied with that?''

''I was hoping you'd do a little investigating. Talk to some people.'' Glancing at her watch, she said, ''I'm due to visit Dad. If you don't mind, you could come along with me. He wants to thank you for helping out. And while we're there, we can get a list of names from him. Springer execs, employees, friends who might know something. While I'm busy at the courthouse, you can try to touch base with as many of them as possible. Take some notes. Find out what people told the police. See if anyone knows or suspects anything that might help us nail the real culprit.''

Rafe knew himself to be one of those people. He had a definite theory about the whys behind the chemical dumping, and he also had what could only be described as a scrap of evidence to back it up. However, hearsay was what the authorities would call it.

Hearsay coming from anyone was, at best, flimsy proof. Coming from an Indian, it would be considered idle talk. Meaningless scuttlebutt. That was why he hadn't gone to the police about what he'd overheard all those weeks ago. And he didn't tell Libby now because he didn't think he could continue working with her if he were to reveal all he knew—all he suspected—and she reacted with doubt and skepticism.

He'd hold his tongue until he knew she trusted him. He'd play his cards close to the chest for now. Focus on digging up more information so he could lay out the pieces of the puzzle for her with simple clarity, with nothing but hard evidence. If real proof of David's innocence was out there, Rafe would find it. And it had to be out there.

"Sounds like a good plan to me," he told her, reaching for his jacket from where it hung on the back of the chair. "Let's go see your father."

David Corbett was sitting alone in the cold, stark interrogation room when Rafe and Libby entered. The metal table was dented, battered, extremely utilitarian. The walls were painted a greenish gray. Drab. Lifeless. Depressing as hell, Rafe decided.

Although his face was clean-shaven, dark smudges underscored David's eyes. His brow was puckered, his jaw tight. He looked like a man with a great deal of anxiety eating at his thoughts.

Libby smiled brightly, hurrying to his side and bending to kiss his cheek.

"Hi, Dad." She set her leather case on the tabletop. "How are you?"

"Fine, hon. I'm just fine." David shifted his attention to Rafe. "Rafe, it's good to see you. Pardon me if I don't get up."

Rafe thought it strange when the man offered him his left hand, but quickly realized that David's right wrist was handcuffed to the arm of the chair he was sitting in. Taking the man's hand in both of his, Rafe pumped it vigorously.

"It's good to see you, sir."

David shook his head. "Stop with the sir stuff, if you don't mind. We're meeting here as friends. At least, I hope we are."

"Absolutely, sir."

Realizing what he'd said, Rafe offered up an apologetic smile and David chuckled.

"Don't you ever doubt it," Rafe added.

"I appreciate your wanting to help my daughter with this mess I'm in."

Darting a quick look at Libby, Rafe saw appreciation glistening in her gaze, and his heart jumped, tendrils of heat curling low in his gut. Her gratitude shouldn't be causing him such satisfaction, but it did.

Warning flags waved in his brain. He wished his reactions to this woman had some sort of switch he could flip off or a cord he could sever.

"Trial location arguments begin tomorrow," Libby informed her father, getting right down to the business at hand. "It could take a couple of days, maybe more, for the judge to make his decision. While I'm busy at the courthouse, I thought Rafe could do a little interviewing." She opened her case and extracted a yellow legal pad and pen. "Dad, can you think of anyone…anyone at all who might shed some light on things?"

She slid the pad in front of her father, handing the pen to him.

Then her brows drew together, moisture instantly shimmering in her eyes, when she evidently realized the handcuffs were going to be a detriment to him. It was so obviously hard for her, Rafe reflected, seeing her father like this. She cleared the emotion from her throat as she reached for the paper.

"How about if I take down the names?"

David placed a quelling hand on the pad. "I'll make do, hon. I'll make do." He picked up the pen in his left hand.

Libby nodded, muttering, "Idiot guards." She rose from her chair, her cheeks flushed with sudden anger, and went to the locked door. She banged on it. Hard. "Can someone come in here? Now!"

A guard appeared and she demanded that her father be released. The guard stiffly informed her that would be impossible. He did, however, agree to switch the handcuffs to David's left wrist. All the while, Rafe sat silent, watching, his protective instinct stirring. However, rising to give the policeman more grief would do nothing whatsoever to help the situation. Once the task was performed, the guard left the room, locking the door behind him.

David was busy writing, but, with his head still bent over the pad, he softly asked, "Should we think about making a bargain?"

"What?"

Rafe heard the sharpness in Libby's tone. Her father refused to lift his gaze from where it was glued to the task at hand.

She reached out and touched David's forearm. "Dad," she said, her voice more pliant, "you don't know what you're saying. We haven't had a chance to view the evidence. We don't know that a plausible case can even be made against you. Why on earth would you want to admit defeat before we've even had a chance to put up a fight?"

Libby seemed to run out of energy suddenly, and Rafe glanced at her. Her expression was…odd. A frown puckered her brow. Concern darkened her eyes. She was gazing off, seeming to wrestle with some troubling thoughts. The urge to reach out to her was powerful, but it was overridden by the strong, abrupt sense that he was being stared at.

David's brown gaze narrowed on him, and Rafe was sure the man was trying to convey a message of some sort. However, when Libby's attention returned to the moment, his head dipped, and he once again began pushing the pen against the paper.

"We can fight this, Dad. We can."

"I know we can, hon."

But Rafe didn't hear much conviction in his words. David's demeanor was strange, Rafe thought. It was almost as if he was convinced that the battle was lost even before it had begun. Not at all like the strong-willed man Rafe had expected David Corbett to be.

"I've done a little reading…"

Rafe only half listened to Libby, his attention homing in on David. Each and every time that the man's daughter turned her gaze away, David would spear Rafe with a sharp, almost desperate look.

"And since the authorities aren't pursuing Springer," Libby continued, "that must mean that the company is cooperating with them against you. I can't believe the upper management creeps would do that to you after all you've given that company."

Once again, with quick, darting glances, David kept indicating the legal pad on which he wrote. Finally, Rafe gave one nearly imperceptible nod to let the man know he understood.

What could David possibly want to convey that he didn't want Libby to know? Libby was his lawyer. She couldn't represent him if she didn't know everything.

Immediately, Rafe thought of the small puzzle piece he'd refused to present. But it wasn't as if he was never going to reveal all to the woman. He simply wanted to wait until he had more solid proof.

"As far as I've been able to tell—" Libby reached into her briefcase and extracted a notebook, flipping it open "—there's not been a precedent set in a case like this. And as hot as environmental issues are these days, it could be that the authorities are thinking of setting you up as an example.''

Frustration flushed David's neck and cheeks. ''But I didn't do anything. I *wouldn't* do—''

''I know that, Dad.'' Her very air become soft and consoling. ''And we'll prove that, too. Where it counts. In court.''

Father and daughter shared a brief silence, and Rafe was left feeling as though he were intruding on a special moment. Then Libby went back to studying her notes.

''One good thing,'' she said. ''Setting a precedent on any issue isn't easy. They've got to have proof. Rock solid. And since you didn't have anything to do with the contamination, then they're going to have a hard time coming up with what they need, now, aren't they?''

It was a rhetorical question, meant only to bolster and encourage.

David tore off the top sheet from the pad, then leaned toward the table, obviously intending to hand the paper to Rafe. But Libby reached for it.

''Thanks, Dad.''

In that instant, Rafe read panic in the older man's expression. Reaching out, he slipped the paper from David's fingers before Libby even had a chance to touch it.

''I'll take care of that,'' Rafe said to no one in particular.

Libby looked a little startled. For a moment Rafe was worried that she'd insist on taking possession of the list her father had compiled. But in the end she seemed to shrug it off.

''Well,'' she said, ''would you mind getting me a copy of those names? For my records.''

Keeping his tone light, he assured her, ''Sure thing.'' He folded the yellow paper into a smaller rectangle and tucked it safely into his breast pocket. However, the list felt as if it were a flaring match, blistering hot against his skin, so badly did he want to discover the secret message David had written.

Not long afterward, Libby and Rafe were heading out of the jailhouse.

"It's upsetting," Libby commented out of the blue. "He seems so depressed, so defeated. I mean, I know he's under a lot of pressure. He was just fired by a company he'd dedicated his whole life to. He's been accused of a horrendous crime, but…"

Her long, slender throat convulsed in a swallow, and Rafe wondered what it would feel like to press his fingertips against her soft, creamy skin. Or better yet, his lips. At once, hormones pulsed through his body, fierce and fervent. He clamped a lid on his runaway libido, forcing his thoughts back to the subject at hand: David's behavior during their visit.

Rafe had thought the same thing about Libby's father's demeanor. There had seemed to be no fight in him. But feeling that Libby needed to hear something a little more heartening, he said, "Once we get our hands on the evidence, once we start talking to people, planning our strategy, he'll perk up."

"I'm sure you're right."

But her sea-green gaze was still clouded with doubt, and he was left wondering what other misgivings were causing her such tremendous anxiety. He'd have loved nothing more than to hug her to him and assure her that everything was going to be all right. But she wouldn't appreciate such an act. And he certainly didn't dare put himself in such a role. It would surely change their professional relationship into something personal. Intimate. And that was something he meant to avoid.

"It's still early," Libby finally said. "I think I'll shoot over to the courthouse."

Rafe nodded, looking at his wristwatch. "I could run home and check on my horses. How about if I meet you back at your father's house in, say, an hour?"

"That sounds good to me."

With a final wave, Libby got into her car and drove away.

Immediately, Rafe reached up and plucked David's list from his breast pocket. The paper was crisp against his fingertips as he swiftly unfolded it. His eyes scanned down the list of names. He found David's message near the bottom, carefully written as if it was just one more name of someone to be interviewed.

Protect Libby.

Four

"So what good does it do us to know that David eats out more than eighty percent of the time?" Rafe commented. "Or that he replenishes his wardrobe like clockwork every six months? Or buys a new car every five years?"

Libby poked her chopsticks down into the white cardboard container and extracted a crunchy snow pea, grinning as she slid it into her mouth and chewed. For someone who wasn't used to this task, studying piles of evidence could be frustrating. Poor Rafe was probably sorry he'd offered to help her. She may have won the argument to have the trial held here in Prosperino, but now she and Rafe faced the daunting task of sorting through the mountain of papers and playing guessing games as to the opposing counsel's strategy.

Once she'd swallowed, she said, "I told you the prosecution would want to look at Dad's finances. They were hoping to find some unexplainable deposits, searching for a secret stash—''

''But there's none of that here. Every penny is meticulously recorded. Every deposit in his bank account is either his salary or his yearly bonus from Springer. It's all accounted for. It's all thoroughly legit. The man is innocent as a newborn lamb. Surely they'll see that.''

Libby knew by Rafe's use of ''they'' that he'd meant the attorneys who were trying to convict her father.

''To them, the only thing this proves,'' she told him, ''is that Dad is smart enough not to deposit unexplained funds in his bank account. For all they know, he's got a big, fat Swiss bank account.''

''If they're allowed to present that line of reasoning,'' he cut in, ''how are we ever to prove his innocence?''

''Proving his innocence isn't our job,'' she explained. ''It's the other side's job to do the proving. Dad's innocent until proven guilty. That's the beauty of the U.S. court system. Our job is to refute any evidence they present.''

''True. But if a man with such an upstanding character as David Corbett can be arrested, then it only shows one thing—this legal system of ours can be unpredictable. It can be crazy.''

She nodded, smiling. ''Yep, I agree. Sometimes it's both those things. But it's all we've got so we'd better decide to work with it.''

He stretched his neck one way, then the other. Then he lifted his arms and reached high, elongating the muscles of his well-formed arms and torso.

It was impossible for Libby to keep her gaze from dipping to his massive chest. Working with Rafe during the evenings as they read over the first batch of evidence that was provided to them was so hard for her. With his long, flowing hair, his powerful build, those amazingly intense mahogany eyes, he was more attractive to her than any other man she'd ever met.

Even Stephen.

And she hadn't imagined ever wanting a man as much as she'd thought she'd wanted Stephen back in her law-school days. The rat! She shut down the dark memories, refused to give them an opportunity to rear their ugly heads. Instead, she focused on the man sitting at the dining room table with her now.

Rafe's eyes were closed, his chin tipped up, as he stretched the kinks from his muscles. My, how she'd love to run her fingers down the naked length of him. She could only imagine how hard, how sculpted his body would feel.

Libby tightened her grip on the chopsticks until she feared they'd snap in two.

"I could use some more wine," she told him. "How about you?"

She stuck the sticks into the now tepid Chinese vegetables and set down the container where it wouldn't stain the papers that were stacked on the table.

"Sure." He got up and turned to go into the kitchen.

Soft blue denim hugged his butt. And what a nice, tight butt it was, too.

Libby grinned. She was being so bad. She knew it, and it was so unlike her.

She was not looking to get involved with Rafe. Her experience in the past had made her resolve not to get involved with *any* man. Relationships were just too painful.

But what harm was there in checking out the view? she wondered, her smile widening.

What she'd really like was to see the slick, black river

of hair flowing free against the bare flesh covering the wide, strong expanse of his muscular back. To feel those silken tresses against her own naked flesh. A loose and languid chuckle rose in her throat and she did her best to stifle it.

"What has you grinning from ear to ear?" he asked, standing in the doorway between the kitchen and dining room, the open bottle of wine in his hand.

Her eyes widened a fraction and she felt a sudden flush of embarrassment at having been caught in the midst of such naughty, purely erotic thoughts. Her smile disappeared in a puff like dry, brittle paper in fire. One instant the extremely carnal imagery was there, the next it was gone.

"Nothing," she told him. She slid her wineglass away from her. "On second thought, I think I've had enough wine for one evening."

He corked the bottle. "Then I should go. It's nearly midnight and you need to be at the courthouse by eight in the morning. I've stayed too long as it is."

After setting the merlot on the table, he reached for his jacket.

"Rafe—"

When his rich russet gaze landed on her, she found it hard to breathe, nearly impossible to speak, so great was the wave of gratitude that suddenly engulfed her.

His eyes held an intensity, a power, a raw force, that she'd never in her life experienced.

What a ridiculous notion, she silently chided herself. The only thing that was wrong with her at the moment was that she'd had too much to drink. She was tired and stressed to the max.

Nevertheless, she was compelled to reveal her thoughts to him.

"I want to thank you. You've been such a great help to me this past week. Without you, I'd have been all alone in this."

For long seconds he just stood there. She found her mind roving over the different opinions she'd formed about him. He was a proud man. And she found that pride to be almost overwhelmingly appealing. He was intelligent and diligent. Detail oriented. He'd worked hard to attain his dream of having a horse ranch. He was self-sufficient, from what she could tell, asking help from no one, although he'd been quick to offer her father assistance when it was needed.

Rafe James was a man to be admired. And Libby was discovering that she might be coming to admire him way too much.

"I'm glad I could help," he said. "I really am."

The very air seemed to hum with some sort of undercurrent, Rafe thought as he stood there, jacket in hand. And the hum was growing louder—and harder to ignore—with each passing day.

She was a stunningly beautiful woman with her sun-fire curls and those amazing aquamarine eyes. And although his body pulsed with desire for her, she had more than mere physical beauty going for her. She was one hell of a lawyer.

When the two of them had first broken into the boxes of evidence provided by the court, she'd angrily lamented that the prosecutor had sent none of the important documents.

"I won't let them get away with these delaying tactics," she'd promised.

And she hadn't, either. She'd filed a complaint with the judge the very next day. A complaint that ultimately caused the judge to lecture the opposing counsel. A chagrined prosecutor had stiffly promised Libby that more of the evidence would be forthcoming.

However, even though Libby seemed so very confident wearing her professional hat, Rafe couldn't deny his suspicions that, deep down inside, she was as fragile as a sparrow, her self-esteem tenuous and delicate. He couldn't say why he felt this way. He just did.

Maybe it was the small, self-deprecating asides she was in the habit of murmuring to herself when she thought no one else was listening. Or maybe it was the doubt that often shadowed her lovely gaze.

Whatever the reason, he knew he was often swamped by the urge to shield her. From the world at large. From the reporters who were so willing to place guilt even before the trial had begun. From the worry of the case. Even from herself and the long hours she insisted on working.

And that inclination to protect her, more and more often, seemed to weave itself amid the potent attraction he felt for her. As the days wore on, he was becoming less able to clearly delineate his feelings. All he had to do was look at her, he was coming to realize, and sentiment churned, his blood heated. Where she was concerned his emotions were becoming mysterious, confused, evocative.

But as complicated as his reaction to her was becoming, he still had every intention of ignoring it. The events in his past had forced him into a certain way of living, a certain way of thinking and feeling. For mere survival's sake.

And Rafe knew he was much too hard for a delicate dove such as Libby.

What he needed to do was disregard the humming current pulsing between them. Pay no heed to the desires of his body. The right thing to do would be to bid her good-night and walk away.

But as he was about to do just that, she said, "I don't think you understand."

Anxiety, dark and spectral, seeped into Libby's blue-green gaze and it tore at Rafe's very soul. Without conscious thought, he lowered the hand that was holding his jacket and the hem hit the floor. He waited.

She swallowed, and it was clear to him that it was taking a great deal of her energy to remain composed.

"I honestly do believe that, without you, I'd be in this all on my own." Pausing, she tucked her full bottom lip between her teeth. "I…I hate to say this. But I just don't think my dad has much faith in me. I think…I really think he doubts my ability to represent him."

His brow puckered. "That's silly, Libby."

Hurt shimmied across her expression and Rafe immediately was sorry for his choice of words.

"What makes you say that?" he asked.

Libby hesitated, and he got the sense that she was debating what or how much to tell him.

Finally, she said, "He didn't want me to come to Prosperino. He used the excuse that this case was sure to get messy and he didn't want my professional name and reputation connected to it. But I just have a feeling…"

Apprehension bathed her beautiful face.

"I just think he doesn't have confidence in me."

The urge to go to her was strong, almost stronger than his will to do what was right.

She needed reassurance. She needed support, comfort, encouragement.

He desperately wanted to give her all those things. The very essence of him called out for him to act.

But doing so would lead him down a road he didn't

want to travel. He'd be wronging her and his own convictions. So, instead, he forced his feet to remain riveted in place and he let a smile soften his features.

"That really is silly," he repeated, this time knowing that his expression kept the words from being hurtful. "Your father is up to his neck in hot water. If he thought you couldn't pull him out before he drowned, he's smart enough to speak up about it. I believe that." Then he added, "You can believe that, too."

Her gaze cleared, and his heart lightened, his blood simmered in his veins.

Great Father above, he was going to need help ignoring the desire he felt for this woman. Lots of help.

His assurances had been gruff at best. But he was relieved that they had been enough to bolster her. At least for the moment.

The night air was nippy as he made his way to his truck. But rather than curse the chill, he thanked fate for the opportunity to cool the need pulsing through him and wake his sleepy senses. He forced the craving he felt for Libby from his mind, from his body, and focused on the important duty awaiting him. Protecting David's daughter.

She had no idea she might be in danger. And if the truth were known, he had little more than gut instinct telling him that she could be the target of someone's nefarious intentions. However, a winter fog was rolling in, misty tendrils creeping along the ground, engulfing bushes, trees, cars. Perfect cover for someone who wanted to remain unseen. He'd have to remain vigilant tonight.

He scrubbed at his face. Lethargy and fatigue wouldn't be his only battles tonight. Images of Libby danced just behind his eyelids. The passionate longing that plagued him would be a formidable foe as well.

As he had every other night this week, he drove his truck down the block, made a U turn, pulled to the curb, cut the engine…and watched.

Usually, Rafe avoided Ruby's Café during peak business hours, but if he didn't get some caffeine into his system this morning he was surely going to crash. Mokee-kittuun folklore was full of brave warriors who could remain alert for days at a stretch without sleep or sustenance. But he suspected those stories were more myth than reality.

"Coffee to go, please," he told the waitress behind the counter.

She nodded and went to fill his order.

Ruby's hadn't changed in all the years that he could remember. The art galleries and antique shops lining Prosperino's streets brought plenty of tourists into town, but if you wanted to mingle with the locals, Ruby's was the place to be.

Not that Rafe was known for going out of his way to mingle. However, that was going to have to change if he wanted to learn anything that might help David.

He rested his forearms on the wooden countertop, waiting for his coffee, when he heard his name called from the back of the room. Sweeping his gaze in that direction, he saw Prosperino's mayor, Michael Longstreet, waving for Rafe to join him.

"Rafe!" the gregarious mayor greeted him, pumping his proffered hand. "How are you?"

"Fine, Michael. Just fine. How about yourself?"

"I'm doing great. Just great." The man's whole expression beamed with happiness.

Although Rafe had only officially met the mayor a few weeks earlier, it was common knowledge that Michael had just gotten married last month. The man had a bit of a playboy reputation in town, and everyone had been surprised when he'd tied the knot.

Politeness had Rafe asking, "How's your wife?"

"Suzanne is great, too," Michael continued. Then he sobered. "She works with the teens at Emily's House out at Hopechest."

The drinking water at the youth ranch had been the first place the DMBE had shown up. The staff and children had been evacuated to Joe Colton's estate, Hacienda de Alegria. Blake Fallon, Rafe's best friend, ran Hopechest Ranch. After just having to deal with the fact that his father tried to murder Joe Colton, Blake hadn't needed more to trouble him.

Even though he and Blake had been friends since childhood, Rafe hadn't yet told him about his suspicions regarding the polluting of the aquifer. The information he had could be misconstrued to make David look even more guilty than he already did. Rafe hoped that, at the end of this mess, all would be revealed and the real guilty party would be apprehended.

"I heard you're working for Libby Corbett," Mayor Longstreet said. "Helping to clear David's name."

"That's right."

Suddenly Rafe felt on edge, which was odd. He guessed it was the negative press David was receiving in the local papers and the national news that had him antsy about the townspeople's reaction to him helping the Corbett family.

"Well, I think you ought to know—" the man's voice lowered "—there's a rumor racing through the courthouse. The prosecutor is thinking of charging David with the death of that EPA employee. The one who was killed in December. His name was Charlie O'Connell.''

Rafe couldn't believe what he was hearing. ''That's ridiculous! I read in the papers weeks ago that O'Connell's death was ruled an accident.''

Michael shrugged, his eyebrows rising. ''That was before the dumping of this DMBE was thought to be deliberate. And there were scratches on the car O'Connell was driving. Paint samples were taken.''

''David Corbett had nothing to do with the DMBE or O'Connell's death.'' Rafe tried to keep his tone down, but the anger running through him made that difficult. ''The man is no murderer!''

The mayor placed a quelling hand on Rafe's shoulder. ''I know that, Rafe. I do. And that's exactly why I'm telling you about the rumor. Forewarned is forearmed.'' Then he added, ''Libby Corbett ought to know what her father is up against.''

Rafe nodded silent thanks. Michael was right. Libby did need to be alerted if more charges were going to be pressed against David.

''You're a lawyer, Michael. How likely is it that they'll pin all this crap on David?''

Worry hooded Michael's green eyes and he shook his head. ''I just don't know. Depends on what evidence they have.''

The sound Rafe emitted was derisive. ''That's just it. The prosecutor says he has a ton of evidence against David. He's told that to everyone who will listen.''

''Yes, I've read it in the paper.'' Michael's dark head bobbed now. ''Seen it on the evening news.''

''Yet, we can find nothing that looks incriminating in the discovery Libby's received. The prosecutor is using every excuse in the book to keep the implicating evidence out of our hands.''

"He's just playing for time, and his stalling tells me that he's not really sure of his case strategy. But he'll soon run out of excuses. Especially if Libby keeps filing those discovery motions and hounding the judge." A shadow of a smile curled the edges of Michael's mouth. "Surprise evidence might generate exciting television drama; however, it paves the way for poor justice. The judge knows that. So do all the attorneys involved. Libby's one hell of a lawyer. She knows what she's doing. She'll eventually get her hands on everything that the opposing counsel has on David."

Rafe saw that the waitress was looking impatient as she stood at the counter with his order. He bid Michael goodbye, thanking him for the information about the new charges David might be facing.

After paying for his coffee, Rafe pushed his way out the door and into the foggy morning, dread sitting in his stomach like a brick at the thought of having to be the bearer of bad news.

Five

"I told Michael it was ludicrous. That David just isn't capable of murder." Rafe set the box of papers on the dining room table with the others they had carried into the house from Libby's car. More copies of documents the police had seized from the house and David's office at Springer.

She sighed wearily. "Well, he hasn't been charged with O'Connell's death yet, so let's not worry about it until it happens."

Automatically he reached to open a box. Libby stopped him by sliding her hand over his.

The heat of her scorched his skin, and his gaze darted from the creamy flesh of her hand to her face. Time seemed to slow until the seconds only slogged by. She, too, was obviously aware that something stirred between them.

Her lovely eyes blinked, then averted, and she snatched

her hand away from his. When her gaze returned to his face, she said, "I thought we should wait…thought we should get something to eat before we dive into this stuff."

"Sure." His voice was a mere whisper, rusty and grating, as awareness of the moment—awareness of her—permeated each and every cell of his being, each and every molecule around him, making the temperature of the room rise, the air grow heavy.

And with the keen perception came desire.

Raw and throbbing.

The need roiling in him was astounding, and it had welled up from nowhere. She saw it, he knew. She was experiencing something akin to it. He realized that, too. Could see it just as clearly as if it were tattooed in plain English across her forehead. He didn't know what to say, didn't know what to do.

On the heels of desire came an awkwardness the likes of which he'd never been subjected to before.

Like a series of storm-churned waves buffeting the Pacific coastline, each emotion hit them, one after the other, fierce and unrelenting. And they stood there, helpless against the onslaught, taking each sensation as it came. Absorbing it. Being filled with it. Taken over by it.

What amazed him was the fact that the extraordinary change, the craving, the unease that swamped the two of them had taken precedence over everything. Even the daunting news that her father may be facing more charges in the very near future.

"I—I'm exhausted," she told him, turning away her gaze again, refusing or unable to look him in the eye. "And I'm starved. I need a break."

Her voice sounded weak to him. That could have been caused by the amazing moments they had both just encountered. But he had seen her fatigue, had been aware that she'd had a rough day at the courthouse, that she needed a few minutes to relax. Instantly, he was engulfed with remorse to think that he'd been pushing to get right to the new evidence they had acquired.

"You're right. Let's go into the kitchen and get something to eat."

She looked at him then, and gratitude laced the edges of her smile.

Once they were in the kitchen, he forced her into a chair. "Sit," he commanded. "What you need is a glass of wine and a few crackers. You can relax while I cook."

Her brows raised.

"Don't look so surprised. I can cook. I've been taking care of myself for a very long time."

His comment seemed to intrigue her, but he wasn't willing to expound on the subject at the moment. He poured her a glass of wine, and once she'd pointed to which cabinet housed the crackers, he put a few on a plate for her and set it on the table as well.

"You said you're starved," he said, after having scanned the contents of the refrigerator, "so time is of the essence. How about a western omelet and toast? It won't be gourmet fare, but it'll fill you up."

She smiled and Rafe felt as if she'd gifted him with some great award.

"Sounds like heaven to me. Especially if I don't have to prepare it."

He diced an onion and some red and green pepper. "So tell me what it was like growing up in this huge house, in this neighborhood. Must have been a great childhood."

"It probably would have been..."

The up-and-down cutting motion of his wrist slowed when she paused.

"...had I been a normal kid."

The blade of the knife stopped. He let it rest against the wooden cutting board and turned to look at her. Deep shadows clouded her gaze, and he knew then that the fairy-tale childhood he'd imagined her having must be just that. A fairy tale. He found himself interested to know about her past. More interested than he knew was seemly or safe.

Before he could question her about what she meant, she shook her head. "But I don't want to talk about me. I'd rather hear about you. What was it like to grow up on a reservation?"

A dark fog swirled around his feet, threatening to rise and swallow him up. His past was the last thing he wanted to talk about. However, he cast another glance over his shoulder and saw that the murkiness he'd witnessed in her eyes a moment before had dissolved.

"I envision lots of freedom. Time spent in the great outdoors. Days filled with games of challenge. Learning to ride bareback, the wind blowing through your hair. Learning to fish and hunt and track."

His brow was furrowed when he turned to face her. Her eyes were bright and her features were relaxed into an expression that was nothing short of sheer bliss. He tried to chuckle, but there was little humor in the sound he emitted.

"Maybe a hundred years ago."

Her eyes snapped open.

"Libby, you're making reservation life sound positively primitive." He heard the hard edge of his tone, but wasn't able to do a thing to quell it. "Mokee-kittuun mothers want to raise poised, mannerly, technically savvy children, just like every other mother in the world."

She swallowed, her spine straightening. "Oh, Rafe, that was so insensitive of me. I'm sorry. It's just that my own childhood was so…limited. I certainly didn't mean to hurt your feelings."

The feelings he was experiencing surprised him. Normally, stereotypical comments regarding his race made him furious. But he knew she had meant no offense.

"It's okay," he told her. "Really." He went on with the task of preparing their meal, certain that doing so was the best way to let her know all was well.

"Actually," he continued, "I spent a good many years growing up here in town." He didn't want to think about those years. Certainly had no intention of telling her about them. In any detail, that was.

"My nohk-han died when I was three."

"Nohk-han?"

Libby rolled the word around on her tongue, her lyrical voice giving the word an almost poetic sound, and a thrill shot through Rafe.

"The word means father in Algonquian."

She smiled. "It's beautiful." Then she sobered. "I'm sorry your dad died when you were so young. Do you remember him?"

Pressing his lips together, he shook his head. He wished…oh, how he wished. He'd have settled for whispery images. Blurry pictures of a dark-haired, dark-eyed man. Pride shining in his gaze. Laughter. Love.

But Rafe had none of these things. He had no memory of his father. None whatsoever.

"That's sad," Libby said. "So sad."

Sidestepping the dark pit of depressing emotion, Rafe carried on with his story.

"Onna moved us into town," he told Libby.

"Onna..." She paused, then queried him with a look. "Onna means mother?"

He nodded. "She took a job as a housekeeper." Tension gathered in every muscle of his body. He was getting too close to the badness. Too close to the foul memories. But he'd dived into the pool of the past. The challenge now would be to swim across without drowning.

"She ended up marrying the man." Pain ached in his jaw. "Curtis James adopted me. My onna had two children while she was with him. My half brother, River, and my half sister, Cheyenne."

Glancing down, Rafe saw that his grip on the knife left his knuckles white. He tried to relax. But it was nearly impossible.

"Onna died giving birth to Cheyenne."

"Oh, Rafe."

But he barely heard Libby's response.

"My sister and I returned to the reservation after that." Rafe remembered the relief he felt the day Curtis James dropped him off with the Elders. But then his years of worry had begun. Worry over his brother.

"But your stepfather kept your brother?"

There was no way Rafe would ever refer to Curtis as his father, in any way, shape or form. He knew for sure that the man had never thought of him as a son.

"Curtis James took River with him, yes."

"That must have been hard. To have your family split up like that."

"Yes." But hard didn't even begin to describe the torment Rafe had suffered agonizing over River's safety.

Seeming to sense the tension in him, Libby changed the subject. "So your name is James because you were adopted. What was your name before the adoption?"

"Running Deer."

Strength took root in him, growing like a mighty oak. Sturdy. Potent. When he'd been in his late teens, and bordering on getting into real trouble with the law, he'd learned from the Elders who raised him that Running Deer was a name to be proud of. That his nohk-han had been a man to look up to. A man of great esteem. A man whose memory should be honored by his only son. Honored with proper behavior. All those years ago, the Elders had touched on the perfect means of taming Rafe's rebellious nature.

"Rafe Running Deer. I like the sound of it."

Coming from her lips, so did Rafe.

Saturday morning was spent reading and categorizing evidence. Finally around eleven, Libby told Rafe that the death of the EPA employee, Charlie O'Connell, was niggling at her mind, keeping her from focusing. Fighting off *attempted* murder was one thing, she'd said; a murder charge was quite another. She decided to visit the local police station to attempt to talk to officers on duty to see what they remembered about O'Connell's death.

If the truth were to be told, Rafe was relieved to have a break. Not from the monotonous reading, but from being with Libby. Her nearness caused an ever-increasing strain in him, like a match touched to a slow burning fuse. You knew an explosion was about to occur. You just didn't know when, or how big the blast would be.

He wanted her. Oh, how he wanted her. And every moment he was with her, his want—his *need*—seemed to escalate.

Rafe dropped Libby off at the police station, and knowing she couldn't be in a safer place, he decided to run out to the rez to feed his horses. But not before stopping in to visit David first.

Ever since the man had passed over that surreptitious plea, Rafe had been wondering what the story was behind it. Could be that David was just being an overprotective father who was worried about his daughter. Could be that David, innocent of these charges, knew as well as Rafe did that the real culprit was still on the loose. But Rafe didn't think that was the case. He had the distinct impression that David Corbett knew more than he was telling anyone. And if that was so, Rafe meant to find out all he could.

Sitting at the table in the visiting room of the jailhouse while waiting for David, Rafe glanced over at the only other occupants of the room. A scruffy teen and a woman Rafe guessed to be the boy's mother.

Although Rafe didn't know the teenager by name, he had seen him trespassing on rez land on a motor bike. More than once Rafe had lately witnessed the young man's angry outbursts with various townspeople and thought of his own rebellious adolescence. Rafe was so grateful that the Mokee-kittuun Elders had taken hold of him with firm but loving hands.

He'd been one angry child when his onna had died and Curtis James had dumped off him and his baby sister at the reservation like sacks of rubbish he no longer wanted.

At first, no one on the reservation seemed to know what to do with the James children. Cheyenne was just an infant and had been taken in by a loving family. Rafe had been ten, a boy with hatred in his heart and anger in his eyes. For six years he'd practically been allowed to run free, and he'd taken every advantage of that freedom. He'd hooked up with a friend, Blake Fallon, a boy whose internal anger matched Rafe's. The two of them had made a great team.

The only time the boys ever felt truly released from the torment of their circumstances was when they were riding. Fast. It didn't matter what they rode, as long as it flew and it had two wheels.

Motorcycles. Dirt bikes. Scooters, plain or fancy.

The fact that those vehicles were stolen upset the law enforcement officers of Prosperino. But for years Rafe and Blake led the police on a merry chase.

The woman's soft sobs had Rafe casting a glance across the room. Up until now the teen had been trying valiantly to put on a defiant face. But his mother's tears were cracking his hard facade, and when the adolescent's eyes welled with emotion, Rafe knew in his heart that there was hope for the boy. The teen's heart hadn't yet turned to concrete. Hopefully, the court system would get the boy into counseling where he belonged.

David arrived in the visitation room, the dark smudges beneath his eyes clear signs that the man wasn't sleeping well.

"How come you're not with Libby?"

Anxiety shaded David's brown eyes.

"She's perfectly safe," Rafe assured him. "I dropped her off at the police station. She wants to do a little investigating. Talk to some people."

The extra murder charges might never be leveled on David, so Rafe felt it unnecessary to worry the man with more detail than that.

"I'm sure she'll come to see you later today."

David only nodded in response. It was so obvious that something was gnawing at the man's thoughts, that Rafe couldn't waste any more time with small talk.

"Look, David, you need to tell me what's going on."

"What do you mean?" The man's expression turned hooded. "How can you ask that? I'm being accused of a crime I didn't commit—"

"With all due respect," Rafe firmly interrupted, "I have to tell you that I think you know more than you're admitting. How can Libby and I help you if you don't tell us everything?"

David's mouth drew into a rigid line.

Rafe softened his tone. "David," he began, "any father would want his daughter protected. I understand that. But there was desperation written all over that paper you handed me the other day. Enough desperation that you didn't want Libby to see it." He leaned forward a fraction. "I'm going to ask you again. What's going on? Something is obviously causing you a great deal of anguish."

Hesitation hovered over David like a miasma. But finally the fear he'd worked hard to conceal focused at the surface. The man's shoulders slumped, and he dipped his head and tossed a quick glance toward the door where an officer stood guard.

"Libby's in terrible danger," David said, his voice low. "And so am I. I'm in trouble, Rafe. Deep trouble."

"From whom? From what?"

David lifted his hands to the tabletop, lacing his fingers tightly, resting his forearms on the metal edge. "I don't know. I don't know who...but I do know why."

Remaining stock still, Rafe listened.

"Back in November, around Thanksgiving," David continued, "I received an anonymous correspondence. I have no idea who sent it. But the message indicated that several barrels of DMBE were missing and it was inferred that the chemical might be illegally dumped."

The older man scoured his jaw with an agitated hand.

"Whoever sent that message to me had to be a Springer employee. And this person was frightened enough that he—or she—didn't want to come forward."

Rafe asked, "Did you tell anyone about the note?"

David shook his head. "Not a soul. And I didn't launch a full-fledged investigation because I didn't know for certain that any wrongdoing had taken place. But I did start looking into the matter. Asking some questions." He paused. "And apparently I must have hit a nerve."

A torrent of apprehension seemed to swirl around David. His brown eyes glistened with fear, his throat tightened with trepidation.

"I received a package in the mail," he continued. "Inside was a necklace that belonged to Libby. A gold pendant she'd inherited from her mother. With it came a warning for me to back off, to forget about the DMBE."

A tiny tremor quivered the man's chin and it took him a moment to rein in the terror that so obviously threatened to overwhelm him.

"Rafe, whoever sent the necklace and the warning had been to San Francisco. *This person was inside my daughter's house.*"

He looked away then, the hand he lifted trembling.

"Heaven help me, but I let the whole thing go unreported." David's gaze was wide, haunted. "I let the matter drop. I hoped and prayed it was an isolated incident." He swallowed. "Rafe, Libby is all I've got in this world. I couldn't let anything happen to her. I just couldn't."

His sigh was shaky. "So I deleted the note I was sent and I never asked another question about it."

Rafe knew that, for an honorable man such as David, letting something like this go wouldn't be easy. The man must have spent the last few months feeling wracked with anguish.

"There was nothing else I could do," he said. "But now the situation has turned even more dire. More of the contaminant is missing and Libby is still in danger." A single tear welled in the corner of his eye and he dashed it away with a swift swipe of his knuckle. "And those poor kids at Hopechest sick. God, Rafe, how I've agonized over this."

He raked shaky fingers through his auburn hair. "Why would anyone want to destroy our water supply? I just can't understand it. It had to be an accident. An accident that someone at Springer wants to blame me for. If they make me the guilty party, then the company could save millions in clean-up costs and punitive damages." He shook his head. "It's the only motive I can think of. The only reason that makes any sense at all…"

David's voice petered out, and the man gazed off across the room.

As Rafe tried to take in everything David had said, there was one point that seared his thoughts. David thought the dumping had to have been an accident. Well, Rafe felt differently.

The pollutant that had seeped into the ground, oozed into the aquifer, had been no accident.

"I should have come forward," David whimpered. "My God, I should have told someone."

"David, the chemical had already gone missing," Rafe reminded him. "It probably had already been dumped by the time you were alerted."

"But I could have warned them."

"Who?" Rafe hoped this most rational question would calm David.

"Those kids at Hopechest, that's who. I could have

warned Blake Fallon. I could have warned the whole town of Prosperino.''

He desperately wanted to reach out to comfort David, but breaking the no-touching rule would only capture the attention of the guard who stood by the door.

''How could you know where the chemical was dumped? How could you know those kids would get sick? You couldn't. You know you couldn't. When someone dumps illegal chemicals, they don't do it where it'll be detected. They go somewhere that's isolated.''

Rafe had spent many sleepless nights wondering just where someone might have dumped the DMBE.

The clouds shadowing David's dark eyes lifted. But only a little.

''Libby can't know, Rafe. She can't know.'' Anxiety ticked in the older man's cheek. ''What would she think of me? How would she feel knowing that her father was aware that someone made off with a dangerous contaminant and he didn't do anything to find out who or why or when?''

David's agitation had the officer on duty skimming his gaze their way.

Rafe said, ''Listen—''

''She'd be ashamed of me. I couldn't stand that. I don't want you to tell her any of this, you hear me? Besides that, I don't want her feeling afraid. I've spent the last several months in cold, stark fear. It's been awful, I can tell you that. I want you to stick with her. I want you to protect her.''

''I will,'' Rafe promised. ''I won't let anything happen to your daughter, David.''

Libby's angelic face appeared in his mind, her fiery tresses, her milky skin, and Rafe felt his insides grow warm.

David's sigh was ragged. "Maybe I should just take the fall for this whole mess. Maybe I should just say I did it. At least then Libby would be safe."

The fury that rose up in Rafe seemed to come out of nowhere when he heard this suggestion. For years he'd been a victim. For years he'd taken the role of fall guy in order to protect his mother and brother from Curtis James's drunken rages. Never again would he be weak. Never again would he be a victim.

And he wouldn't allow David Corbett to be a victim, either.

"You're not going to do that, David." The edge honing his tone made the elderly man lift his gaze to Rafe's. "You're not going to be held responsible for something you didn't do. I'm committed to clearing your name. And so is Libby. I don't want you to worry about her. I'm going to watch out for her. I'm going to keep her safe."

Taking a small pad of paper from his breast pocket, Rafe asked, "Now, I need some names. When you found out about the DMBE, who did you talk to? And who might have found out that you suspected there was a problem?"

As David began to spout off names, Rafe took meticulous notes and asked many questions.

Six

He saw her standing outside the door of the police station. Her gaze searched up one side of the street and then down the other. She glanced at her wristwatch. This was the first time he'd spotted her where she wasn't either surrounded by lawyers and clerks at the courthouse, or shadowed by that damned Indian she'd hired.

Even though he hadn't gone near the place, he knew she'd been staying at her daddy's house. He didn't want to get caught within a mile of David Corbett's home. Not now. Not while everything was working out so well. Everything Corbett had worked for was about to be destroyed. And best of all, with plans falling so neatly into place, Corbett would spend a good many years in a cold, stark prison cell.

A thin fog hazed the afternoon, and the gray sky was beginning to spit rain.

He'd read in the papers how Libby Corbett had staked

her career on clearing her daddy's name. She had moxie, he had to give her that. But she'd best be careful. There was a fine line between spunk and nosiness. She just might get herself hurt. Or worst yet, killed.

Charlie O'Connell had crossed that line. Once.

Pleasure coursed through him, and amusement curled the corners of his cruel mouth. Without thought, he lifted his hand, swiping his fingers against his lips as if to obliterate any outward sign of humor. The pleasure, he allowed himself to enjoy. It was inside. Safe. Unobservable.

David Corbett may be stupid and weak, but he sure had sired a beautiful daughter.

The image of her sleeping was one he'd never forget. He'd been annoyed that he'd had to travel all the way to San Francisco. But the trip had been well worth his effort.

Her hair had spilled across the pristine white pillowcase, the moonlight streaming through the window turning it to night fire. Her skin had looked like velvet, her lashes fanning against her creamy cheeks. Her long body had been laid out on the bed for his eyes alone. He'd spent long moments in the quiet enjoying the sight of her.

The curve of her shoulder. The swell of her breasts, the dusky disks of her nipples creating shadows against the soft white satin of her gown. He'd actually salivated and grown rock-hard in his trousers.

Had he been a sexual deviate he might have acted on the urges that had pulsed through him that night. But he was no pervert.

He'd focused on his goal, then. Taken what he'd come after—the necklace that had shut David up—and then he'd turned to leave. But not without a final look.

He remembered how innocent she'd seemed. And that

was what he'd derived the most pleasure from. She had lain there sleeping, dreaming, never for a moment imagining her home had been invaded or that danger was so near. That the course of her whole future was, in that instant, at the whim of someone else. Someone more powerful than she.

Exasperation skipped across Libby Corbett's beautiful features as she stood in the foggy mist. Whoever she was waiting for was late. Should he offer her a ride? Interacting with her might prove interesting.

But when he saw her being approached by a woman he knew to be a reporter for the local paper, he was glad he'd remained in his car. He lowered the window several inches, hoping to overhear their conversation, but he was too far away to hear clearly. An errant phrase here and there was all he could make out.

"Environmental Protection Agency…attempted murder charges…chemical contamination…water treatment… DMBE…David Corbett."

Suppressing another smile, he let the warm contentment settle over him. This was just what he'd worked for. He wanted Corbett's name attached to all those horrible and derogatory things. The people of Prosperino might have thought of the high and mighty Corbett as an upstanding citizen. Until now.

His whole body froze when he heard the name "O'Connell" float to him on the heavy, humid air.

Who had uttered it? Libby Corbett or the reporter?

A silent but filthy expletive exploded in his brain.

O'Connell's death had been ruled an accident. That fervor had died down weeks ago. What the hell was Libby Corbett doing bringing it up? Is that why she'd visited the police station?

Fury, white and searing hot, roiled in him. Pain shot

through his head. Red splotches burst behind his eyelids. His gaze narrowed. When he glared at Libby Corbett, he no longer saw a spirited beauty. He saw a meddling bitch who deserved to die an agonizing death.

"Look," Libby told the woman, trying hard to keep a handle on her anger, "I don't have anything else to say."

"But wouldn't your father like for the people to hear his thoughts on what's going on?"

Libby actually laughed. "Good try."

But the woman refused to relent. "What about the rumor of these new charges?"

"I don't comment on rumor." Libby didn't bother trying to keep the irritation out of her voice. "And neither should you. In fact, if you print information based on such a rumor, I will issue a formal complaint with the publisher of your paper. No new charges have been leveled on my client. If my client is charged with something else, I'll be happy to talk to you about it. Now I'd really like it if you'd just leave me alone."

She wheeled away from the reporter and started off down the street. Home wasn't all that far away, she decided. Her shoes felt squishy from the rain, and she realized now that she should have grabbed a slicker from the closet rather than this sweater that sat damp and heavy on her shoulders.

Where was Rafe? He'd promised to pick her up. She was agitated. And she'd been addled by the reporter broaching the subject of O'Connell's death. How had she known that Libby had gone to the station to ask questions about the man's fatal accident?

Lord, the newspapers were going to have a field day if the media suspected that her father might be accused of the premeditated killing of the EPA employee.

Maybe the reporter hadn't really heard anything. Maybe she had simply been grasping at straws. Maybe she'd made a wild guess. Reporters were known to do such things. In fact, a journalist's ability to anticipate a story before his or her colleagues was what separated the good correspondents from the mediocre ones.

In Libby's line of work, she'd dealt with her fair share of media persons, and she knew in her heart that the reporter who had just accosted her would keep nibbling and grinding away until she had herself a story.

An aggravated sigh rushed from her. She was annoyed with Rafe for not returning to the station for her when he said he would. She was annoyed with the reporter. And she was annoyed by the information she'd discovered about Charlie O'Connell's death.

Sgt. Kade Lummus had been open and frank with Libby. O'Connell's car crash had been ruled an accident. However, there had been plenty of questions surrounding the whole incident—questions that, to this day, remained unanswered.

She wanted to discuss the information with Rafe.

Rafe. The thought of how he was making her walk home in the rain made her smolder all the more. And she was still fuming minutes later when she pushed the key into the dead bolt on the front door.

She was wet. She was tired. Her feet hurt like the dickens. And the grumbling of her stomach reminded her that she'd skipped lunch. She kicked off the sopping leather pumps and slid out of her soggy sweater. Deciding she wasn't in the mood to cook, she made up her mind to go out and pick up some burgers for her and Rafe's dinner.

He'd feel bad enough for having stood her up at the police station. Once he found out she'd gotten drenched while walking home and then turned around and driven out to pick him up something to eat, he'd feel like a real heel.

A grin threatened to soften her anger when she imagined the contrition she just might witness in Rafe's intense dark gaze. Most often those mahogany eyes of his were hard as flint and he looked as if he was harboring a thousand secrets.

Solving the puzzle that was Rafe James intrigued her to no end. Even though she had no desire whatsoever to be captivated by him—or any other man for that matter—she'd be lying to herself if she said the urge to figure him out, crack the shell he seemed to be hiding in, didn't intrude on her thoughts, on her dreams.

He was fiercely proud of who he was. Of where he'd come from. But something tormented him. Something in his head, in his past. She could see it, feel it, and it made her wonder...

Libby shook her head to clear her thoughts as hunger pangs rumbled in her belly. She slipped her feet into dry shoes and grabbed a rain slicker from the hall closet. She'd expelled enough energy on Rafe. Right now she wanted to satiate her appetite for food.

Luckily, she'd closed the door of her sedan just before the sky opened, dumping a torrent of rain from the steely clouds. She backed out of the drive and headed out of town in the direction of her favorite burger place.

To an out-of-towner, Jake's probably looked like a real dive. But many people of Prosperino knew that the tiny restaurant was always filled with luscious aromas and friendly faces. In this day and age of healthier eating choices, she wondered how Jake's, with its greasy hamburgers smothered with thick slabs of cheddar cheese, stayed in business, but somehow it did.

She'd order two of the special sirloin burgers with the

works and an extra large serving of the trademark seasoned baked potato wedges. The restaurant was a bit out of the way, but the food was well worth the drive. Rafe would be getting a treat tonight.

The wiper blades slapped a steady, lulling beat, and she began thinking about the hot shower and dry clothes that were waiting for her when she returned home. About the glass of red wine she'd enjoy with her burger and spicy fries in front of a toasty fire. About how she'd razz Rafe for leaving her stranded in the rainy March chill...

When the car that had been following her pulled out and made to pass her, she murmured, "Idiot kid."

No one but a young, inexperienced driver would try to pass in weather like this. The rain made the oncoming cars nearly impossible to see. Instinctively, Libby took her foot off the gas pedal, allowing gravity to slow her car. But the driver of the dark automobile cut back into her lane much too soon, its brake lights blaring bright red.

Her foot stomped the brake pedal and she cut the steering wheel hard to the right. The roar of sound and vibration seemed to block out all thought.

The squealing of the tires. The rumble of loose gravel. The nauseating motion of the rear of her car sweeping violently, veering out of control as she careened off the road, bumping over uneven ground.

The impact caused the air bag to burst out from the steering wheel. Then pain knifed through her skull when her head hit the side window.

Dazed, Libby sat there a moment before she realized it was over. All was still. The jarring, disjointed sounds had ceased, and all that could be heard was the relentless beat of the rain against the roof of her car, the steady thump of the wiper blades on the windshield.

The deep, slow inhalations she pulled into her lungs helped to calm her. But her whole body felt weak and glutinous, as if all her muscles had turned to warm rubber.

She pulled the handle of the car door, but it only opened about four inches before metal grated sharply against metal. Rain pattered against her face, and when she turned her head, a dull pain throbbed up through her temple. Nausea swam in her stomach.

A car pulled to the side of the road and Libby heard the sound of a car door slamming shut as someone got out. A face peered through the crack of her door and a woman shouted, "You okay?"

Libby tried to nod. "Are the others okay?"

"Others?" she asked, pushing her nose a little closer. Only a slice of her features showed. "You're not alone?"

"I'm alone," Libby said. "I mean the people in the other car. A dark car. A kid was driving." Her stomach rolled, and she murmured, "Must have been a kid."

"There's nobody here but you. Now you sit still. Help is coming. I've already called 911 on my cell phone."

Libby glanced out the windshield and saw that whatever she'd hit had made her hood fly open. And the driver side of the car was mangled to the point that the door wouldn't open.

She sighed, resting her aching head against the seat back.

"All this for one of Jake's sirloin burgers."

Seven

The automated doors opened and Rafe rushed into the emergency room of Prosperino Medical Center. Worry had turned into tiny mice that had nibbled at his mind ever since he'd been forced to call the police station to let Libby know that he'd be late picking her up. The officer who had answered the phone assured Rafe that he had Libby in sight and would give her the message.

But Rafe had come to know Libby and he suspected that her inherent impatience wouldn't allow her to wait for him for very long. When he'd arrived at the station to find Libby nowhere to be seen, his worry had turned to icy fear. Especially since he'd heard David's blood-chilling story.

Who could have blackmailed David all those weeks ago, threatened him to keep silent about the illegal dumping in order to keep his daughter safe. Most likely the same person who was responsible for the DMBE contamination of the local aquifer. No other theory would make much sense. But was just one person behind all this, or was there a group involved? He, Libby and David could be facing a whole band of subversives, a single person with a twisted mind, or someone who was completely sane yet cold and calculatingly intent on a single purpose. Not knowing exactly what they were up against was daunting.

What the hell had Libby been doing out on the highway headed out of town?

He stopped at the front desk. "I got a call," he told the receptionist, "that Libby Corbett was brought in."

"Yes, sir," the woman said. "She's in examining room B. Are you family?"

She eyed him up and down, and Rafe was suddenly conscious of his dark skin, hair and eyes. There was no way he could be taken as part of the auburn-haired, Caucasian Corbett clan. His spine straightened, and the familiar feelings of resentment and frustration simmered in the pit of his gut. The officer who had called him had said that Libby was fine, but no one was going to keep Rafe from seeing with his own eyes that she was okay. Without another word, he headed toward Exam Room B.

"Sir!" But her attempt to detain him was halfhearted at best as the phone by her elbow rang and she turned her attention to answering the call.

Nurses and doctors were coming and going but at an unhurried pace. Just as in every other hospital in the country, the sharp scent of antiseptics hung in the air. One young woman sat staring at a computer screen, nibbling on some crackers as she input information. A disembodied female voice hailed a doctor, and then an orderly, over the intercom. A technician backed out of one cubicle, nearly colliding with Rafe, the small tray of blood-filled tubes he carried rattling with his abrupt halt.

"Sorry," the young man said, obviously distracted, his gaze focused on some point at the far end of the hallway.

"No problem." But he'd rushed away too quickly to even hear Rafe's response.

The sight of her sitting there on the bed caused relief to flood through him. He hadn't felt that kind of dizzying lightness in…well, in many, many years. It was the same kind of sensation he'd experienced each and every time he'd had to leave his mother and brother alone with Curtis James. Rafe would invariably return with his heart in his throat until he saw them, touched them, knew that they were safe and sound.

"Libby."

Although he tried to hide the emotion churning inside him, the fear and relief he felt must have registered on his face or in his voice, for her gaze took on that look, the one meant to reassure and assuage.

"I'm fine," she said. Then she repeated, "I'm just fine."

"I'm Kade Lummus." The officer who had been talking with Libby reached out his hand to Rafe.

"I was the one who called you."

"Thanks," Rafe said, shaking the man's hand. Lummus looked to be in his midthirties, tall and tough. Not a hair on his head was out of place, and his uniform looked crisp despite the rainy day. Rafe suspected that nothing got past those perceptive brown eyes of Lummus's.

"I appreciate the call." Rafe directed his gaze at Libby. "What happened? Where did you go? Didn't you get my message? I asked you to wait—"

"Whoa." Libby held one hand up, palm out. The

other, she pressed to the side of her head. "Slow down. You're making my head hurt."

He saw the cold pack sitting on the bedside table, and anxiety shot through him. She had been hurt. Damn it. He hadn't kept her safe like he'd promised David. Like he'd promised himself.

"I did get your message," Libby told him. "And I did wait." Her full mouth quirked up at one corner, pointedly. "For over an hour."

Irritation laced the edges of her tone, but the frailty of it told him that time had diminished its intensity.

"When I went out onto the street to look for you, I was verbally molested by a reporter."

Her gorgeous gem-colored eyes closed for a moment.

"I just couldn't take it," she said, her weariness showing. "So I walked home."

The arch of her brows silently asked his whereabouts.

"I was held up at the ranch. One of my horses isn't well. I had to call a vet and wait for him to show up." The concern in her expression had him hurrying to tell her, "The horse is going to be just fine." After a moment's hesitation, he said, "But the question is, are you?"

"Just a little bump on the head." Reaching up, she touched the left side of her skull. "I was telling Sergeant Lummus here that it had to be some kid. Someone with no driving experience. No one would have tried to pass in such a heavy downpour. You could hardly see the headlights of oncoming traffic."

Lummus looked at Rafe. "The passerby who called for help didn't see anyone else on the road. But like Ms. Corbett said, it was raining pretty hard. Visibility was hampered."

"Did you get the plate number?" Rafe asked Libby.

She shook her head.

"Make or model of the car?"

Another shake of her head.

"Color?"

"Dark" was all she was able to provide.

"She said it could have been any color," Lummus provided. "Navy, green, black, even dark gray." The sergeant looked at Libby and grinned. "You haven't given me much to work on."

"I know," Libby said. "And I'm sorry. But it all happened so fast."

"What were you doing out there?" Rafe asked her again.

One of her eyes narrowed. "I was going to pick up your dinner." Then her shoulders slumped. "Okay, okay. I was starved," she confessed. "I was going after a couple of Jake's sirloin burgers. And then that idiot kid tried to pass me and ended up causing me to have an accident."

That was no accident. Rafe would have bet his prized horses on that. And he was just as sure the driver hadn't been an inexperienced kid who didn't know what he was doing. Libby's near disaster had been calculated. There was no doubt in his mind.

"One good thing will come out of this, though," Libby continued. "Jake will get some free publicity out of all this brouhaha. I told the newspaper reporter that Jake's was my favorite burger joint and that's where I was headed." She chuckled. "Maybe I'll get a free dinner for my trouble." She grinned.

"I don't think this is very funny." Rafe tucked his fist into the pocket of his jeans.

"I know. I know." She cut her eyes at Lummus. "Not

to change the subject, but the sergeant here was good enough to talk to me for quite some time this afternoon.''

The strangest sensation vibrated in Rafe's chest, almost as if he was feeling vaguely threatened. He'd known Libby was going to the station to get what information she could on the death of the EPA employee. Rafe had dropped her off there himself. But discovering that she'd spent the afternoon hours with this officer, he was struck with the oddest feeling...

Kade Lummus nodded. "At the station I heard about Ms. Corbett's accident and I went right to the scene. I told the officers who were there that I knew her and that I'd follow her to the hospital and take her statement.''

Jealousy. Is that what he was feeling?

Not just no, but *hell, no*!

"I think I've got everything I need for my report, so I'll be heading out now.''

Again Lummus smiled at Libby, and Rafe felt his chest huff with...annoyance. Protectiveness. No...covetousness.

If his emotions had been visible at the moment, the green blob that sat in his belly like a concrete block would not be a pretty sight. He knew it.

He heaved a deep inhalation, trying to shove away the unhealthy yet powerful feelings.

Lummus said to Libby, "I'll mail you a copy of the report.''

She grimaced. "I'll need it, I'm sure. My insurance company isn't going to be happy about this missing driver who, as I'm claiming, is at fault here.''

"You take care of yourself." The officer nodded at Rafe. "Good to meet you." With that said, the man was gone.

Rafe stood in the examining room, and although he

knew in his heart he should keep his thoughts to himself, he could no more stop the words from tumbling off his tongue than he could stop his lungs from drawing breath.

"I was scared to death when I got to the police station and I couldn't find you."

The bewilderment she felt was made plain in the frown that creased her brow, in the gently down-turned corners of her mouth.

"Why should you be afraid for me?"

What could he say that wouldn't reveal everything? His intent to protect her from the very beginning? David's bone-chilling story of threat and blackmail? The man's fear for his daughter's safety?

Rafe might have to give himself away. But he didn't have to betray David's trust in him.

Finally he admitted, "I've been worried about your safety from the beginning."

Her confusion deepened along with the pucker between her eyes.

"I told you that I thought David was safer in jail than he would be out walking the streets," he explained further. He let his gaze settle on her. "Well, you're out walking the streets."

Her chest expanded with a silent gasp. "You think this wasn't an accident? But that's just plain silly."

"Silly or not, I want to change our base of operations. I want to take you to Crooked Arrow."

"The reservation? But...why? I'm perfectly safe—"

"There are people I trust there. My ranch is surrounded by lots of open space. It wouldn't be easy for someone to get at you there."

"But, Rafe—" her tone exposed just how ludicrous she thought his idea to be "—don't you think that's going overboard? I understand how you think Dad might be in danger, but I'm his lawyer—''

''You're also his daughter.''

Her jaw snapped shut, her eyes going wide. ''You don't honestly believe someone would try to get at my father through me, do you?''

The question led them too close to the whole truth.

I don't want her feeling afraid. Rafe remembered David's words.

''Let's just say I'd like to play it safe.''

''Well, I still say this was an accident.''

But he saw worry clouding her beautiful aquamarine eyes. And he couldn't help but recognize the similarities between Libby's ''accident'' and the death of the EPA employee. He'd read all about O'Connell's accident in the papers. The car the man had been driving had careened off the road in the rain, when visibility was low and the roads were slippery.

Libby could have been killed.

A knife slashed through Rafe, its blade arctic-cold. He wouldn't let that happen. He wouldn't.

Almost as if she'd sensed his silent comparison of the two car wrecks, Libby said, ''Sergeant Lummus told me that there were plenty of unanswered questions regarding the death of Charlie O'Connell. They have some paint chips from the car's bumper. White.''

Her gaze connected with his when she mentioned the color and Rafe got the distinct impression that she was desperate to defend her thoughts that her accident was just that, an accident. Well, he didn't mind allowing her that. But he refused to let her throw caution to the wind.

''You'll come to the rez?''

Vigilance really was the main reason he pushed. His home would be a safe haven for her. But saying caution was the only reason he pressed her to go would have been a lie. He wanted to get her away from Prosperino. Away from the fancy trappings of this modern age. He wanted to show her how wonderful life could be with a slower pace, a more attuned focus on the world at large. He wanted to see her relax. He wanted to see her on the back of a horse, the wind flowing through her flame-colored hair.

After a moment, she looked off toward one corner of the curtained cubicle, but slowly she nodded. And Rafe's heart soared.

Crooked Arrow Reservation was a most captivating place, and Libby couldn't quite put her finger on why. The landscape that surrounded Rafe's modest brick ranch house was the same lush rolling terrain as she saw in the countryside of Prosperino. Rafe told her that the reservation actually reached far up into the hills.

As she stood by the fence that penned in some beautiful Appaloosas, she surveyed the horizon. A ribbon of vibrant magenta cut a wide swath through the twilight sky. The storm had rolled to the east, leaving the air crisp and fresh. Everything was so open here, so free. Miles away, she spied the home of Rafe's nearest neighbor.

She heard no traffic, saw no people. The isolation gave her a tremendous sense of liberation, of boundlessness. An unrestrained abandon she'd never before experienced.

Anything could happen here.

The thought seemed to whisper from the very depths of her mind, and she smiled.

She truly didn't feel she was in any kind of danger. But she was actually thrilled with the idea of coming to Rafe's home. If she were ever to gain a deeper understanding of the man, this was the place that would offer her that opportunity. Here she could feel free to ask him about his heritage. Here he would feel impelled to teach her about his culture.

Rafe was proud to be Mokee-kittuun. And that deep sense of pride allured Libby. Terribly. It made her want to know all there was to know about the Native American way of life.

Hearing the scuff of his boots against pebbles, she turned. He nodded a silent greeting, his long hair falling free over one shoulder, and then offered her one of the two mugs of steaming tea he carried.

"Thanks." The sweet aroma wafted warmth over her chilled cheeks as she lifted the mug to sip.

"We won't have the room here that we had at David's house," Rafe said. "But the boxes of evidence are all arranged just as you had them."

"I'm sorry I wasn't more help."

"No problem. Maybe the hospital should have kept you more than just one night. Anyway, I was glad you agreed with my suggestion that you have a rest. How's your headache?"

"I'm feeling better, thanks. Almost good as new."

A strange awkwardness had crept between them ever since they had crossed the border onto Crooked Arrow. She guessed it was part of the magnanimous mystique of the reservation she'd been pondering just before he'd made his appearance. Since they had first met, Libby had come to like Rafe. Respect him. She certainly was grateful for all his help. And he attracted her like a moth to a flame. But since arriving on the rez late this afternoon—since stepping onto his territory—she'd begun to feel acutely aware of him, keenly attentive to his every move, his every word and gesture.

She had lain on the double bed in his small guest room,

but sleep would not come. Instead, she'd listened as he'd moved around the house. For quite some time he'd carried in the boxes they had brought from her father's house, the front door opening and closing in the effort. He'd shifted and arranged the boxes, and she assumed he was taking great care to organize them for her. She'd heard water running in the kitchen and imagined him filling a cup and drinking from it, his long hair flowing down his back, his chin tipped up, his strong fingers gripping the glass.

And then she'd begun supposing how those long, tapered fingers would feel against her skin. Her heart had begun to pound and her blood had turned thick with—

That was when she'd pushed herself off the mattress, made her way quietly down the hallway and slipped out the front door.

She and Rafe stood by the fence and drank their tea, enjoying the sunset and the quiet. What notions were roving around in his head? What was he thinking?

She pondered the sense of freedom she'd noticed before he'd arrived with the tea, and sidling it up next to the heightened awareness she was feeling for Rafe, she couldn't help but think that this time spent at Crooked Arrow reservation could get her into deep trouble. Deep trouble, indeed.

But for some odd reason, the idea didn't seem to bother her too much.

Rafe tossed and turned into the wee hours of the morning, the ticking of the bedside clock driving him to the very edge of sanity. Bringing Libby here had been a mistake. Necessary and completely unavoidable. But a mistake, nonetheless.

The woman consumed his every thought.

Those vulnerable gem-colored eyes called to him. That curly thatch of fiery hair glowed golden red in the firelight. Her creamy skin tempted him to reach out and run his fingers down the length of her throat, feel the satin texture of her flesh. Her luscious mouth, moist and full, beckoned for his kiss.

He'd never be able to keep his hands off her. Never.

Jerking the blanket aside, he stood, stretched and then strode to the window. The winter air chilled his naked skin as he gazed out at the starry night, aware of nothing his gaze lit upon.

Dinner had been a strained affair. They had cooked together, eaten together, even cleaned up the dishes together. Conversation had been tense at best. However, he had succeeded in calming the heat in him long enough to tell her how he'd scrimped and saved the money it cost him to acquire his first pair of breeding Appaloosas from a man on a Nez Percé reservation in Washington state. She'd hung on his every word. And he'd truly enjoyed the attention she'd showered on him.

But the entire time they spent together, first in the kitchen preparing and eating dinner, then in the living room by the fire sharing a glass of wine, it had been as though some ghostly entity had been hovering, just waiting to swoop down on them and devour them whole.

He'd experienced the feeling before. At Libby's house. But this time it was stronger. More insistent, urgent.

The attraction he'd felt for Libby had grown so much more intense. Seemingly in the blink of an eye. His need had grown concentrated. Powerful. One moment, it had been a minor torment he'd been sure he could control. The next, he wasn't at all certain that he could restrain the desire raging through his veins.

His goal in bringing her here had been to keep her

safe. And now that he'd gotten her to Crooked Arrow, he was confident that he could protect her from whatever unseen or unknown enemies might be lurking out there, threatening to harm her.

However, with every second that ticked on that god-forsaken clock on the nightstand, he grew less and less sure that he could shield her from what could turn out to be the worst enemy of all.

Himself.

Eight

Libby's heart fluttered a staccato beat as she slipped through the house, squinting to see in the dim morning light. The sun had yet to rise, but the rosy radiance glowing from the windows was a telltale sign that it soon would.

During the three days she'd been in Rafe's cozy home, she had crept from her room each morning, tiptoed down the hall and into the kitchen to peer out the window. To her, the morning ritual he performed looked more a spiritual observance than a religious one. She didn't know if he prayed or meditated out there on the lawn.

The first morning she'd witnessed him had been an accident. She'd come into the kitchen to make coffee and just happened to spy him sitting cross-legged on the blanket, his spine straight, his massive shoulders square, his upper torso bare, his glorious hair unbound, his strong arms outstretched to the sky. The sight had seemed so sacred that she'd told herself to turn away and allow him his privacy. But he had so enthralled her that she had been simply unable to tear her eyes away.

Her nights here had been agonizing. Haunted by erotic dreams of Rafe, she tossed and shifted beneath the blankets, her skin burning under his illusory, wraithlike touch. The night visions never failed to awaken her several times, her heart pounding, her skin damp, before morning would finally arrive and she could scramble from her bed and race to spy on this almost ethereal rite he performed daily.

Now she was held rapt by the sight of him, just as she'd been every other morning. When he finally stood and lengthened his muscular body toward the heavens, Libby knew his meditations were complete and he'd be coming inside soon. She busied herself putting ground beans and water into the coffeemaker and flipping on the machine.

He entered through the back door, greeting her with a smile, and Libby felt her heart *ka-chunk* against her ribs. He was such a handsome man, and the attraction that swirled and danced around them when they were together was unmistakable. Undeniable. Like a lazy waltz that had progressively escalated into a frenzy, Libby knew the magnetism between them was building, becoming stronger and stronger.

Waltz? No. This was more like a tango. A hungry, sexy, completely carnal need that was just waiting to consume them. The real question in Libby's mind was just which one of them would be the first to succumb to the overwhelming force of it.

"Morning."

She smiled a tight greeting. Why did he have to walk around half-naked? There was pride in his straight spine.

Not a look-at-me kind of pride. This was more an inner dignity that simply couldn't be missed.

That heavy awkwardness settled over her. Over them both.

"You're welcome to join me, you know."

Her cheeks flamed red hot and she was relieved that he'd turned away to fold the handwoven blanket he used every morning.

"Join you?"

Oh, my. He wasn't really aware that she watched him, was he? But how? His back was to her each morning. And she was always careful to move from the window when he rose and stretched.

"It's good to give thanks. I'm grateful for all I have. I like to take the time to actually think it and say it."

She was grateful. Grateful that he wasn't pressing the issue of her voyeurism. She made a silent vow to grant him some solitude tomorrow. But even as she made the promise to herself, she knew the next morning would find her once again at the kitchen window, her weak will having surrendered to the urge to observe him.

"The Great Spirit deserves thanks."

Shyly she asked, "Does The Great Spirit have a formal name to your people?" She wanted to hear him speak in his native tongue.

"Kit-tan-it-to'wet."

The lyric syllables rolled from his lips like soft music, and a shiver coursed across Libby's skin.

"The Great One has blessed me in many ways," he told her. "And I feel compelled to show my appreciation each morning."

With a silent nod and a small smile, she agreed with him, with his philosophy of cultivating an essence, a core, of gratitude.

Then almost of its own volition, her gaze slid from his honed cheekbones, the hollows of his cheeks, his strong jaw, to his smooth chest. His stomach was flat, the muscles rolling in true washboard fashion. Night after night she'd fantasized about running her fingers over those hills and valleys, dreamed about what his strong, demanding hands would feel like on her own body.

Libby dragged air into her lungs and forced her eyes to lift to his face. His mahogany gaze had narrowed. He knew. He knew the carnal thoughts that filled her mind. She realized it…could feel it in her bones.

Embarrassed beyond measure, she wheeled around, meaning to reach for the coffeepot. But she miscalculated the distance and ended up touching her knuckle to the edge of the heating element under the pot.

She gasped, jerking her hand to her chest.

Rafe was at her side in an instant.

"Here," he said, gently taking her hand in his. "Let me see."

He was so close. Too close. The warm male scent that was his alone enveloped her like a warm wool blanket, and she fought the urge to close her eyes and revel in it. Up close, his swarthy skin was lustrous. Smooth. Flawless. And she ached to splay her palm against his broad chest, feel the beat of his heart, experience the warmth of him.

Guiding her to the sink, he flipped on the water and plunged her hand into the cold cascade. She was barely conscious of the chilled temperature, barely conscious of the burn on her finger. The only thing she was cognizant of was him. The solid mass of him standing just inches from her.

Their gazes clashed, and his voice was whisper-soft as

he said, "It's so strange, isn't it? Like a living, breathing thing."

He was describing the allure they felt. And, God help her, she knew he spoke the truth. It would be so easy to just let go, to let her very soul become possessed by the surreal entity of the attraction that plagued them, to lean forward, lift up on tiptoes and press her mouth to his. It would take so very little effort to relax against the hard length of him, to let desire have reign. But a fear welled up in her chest, an icy, bitter fear that had her inching away from him.

"I can't." The words were like sandpaper, grating against her throat as she spoke them. And she could only hope he would understand her meaning.

He was a man of few words, Rafe was. He was contemplative. Deep thinking. She'd learned that much about him. But he'd shown her, over and over, that he had a tender side. A gentle nature.

No matter how kindhearted he might be, Libby simply would never be able to open herself to another man. Not after the way she'd been used and then tossed aside so callously.

Love hurt. She knew that, had experienced it firsthand. She'd exposed her emotions and thoughts, given of herself, wholly, freely, only to have the gift of her love mocked by the very man she'd thought she'd cared for. She wasn't ready to feel that kind of pain again. In fact, she didn't think she'd ever be ready.

A sigh tore from his chest. His tone was gruff as he said, "That's good. Because I can't, either."

His past wasn't any of her business. But she couldn't help feeling curious about his comment. There was great impetus behind the fortifications surrounding her own heart. But what could have happened to him to make him throw up those protective walls that encircled his?

He turned off the water, reached for a soft cotton dish towel and lightly patted her hand dry.

"I think you're going to live." The pitch of his voice was now light, teasing. He made to step away from her. "I should go have a shower."

Although every fiber of her being screamed that it was a mistake, Libby reached out and stopped his retreat with one light touch of her fingers on his corded forearm.

An awkward moment pulsed thickly by. Finally, she said, "Your sister Cheyenne…does she still live on the reservation?"

A shining strand of his long hair fell over his shoulder, cascading down his chest as he shook his head from side to side. "She lives and works at Hopechest Ranch. She counsels the kids there. She's married to Jackson Colton."

Libby's eyes widened a fraction. The whole fantastic Colton story had made the San Francisco newspapers.

"Do you think I'll get to meet them while I'm here?"

"I don't see how you'll avoid it."

He grinned, but he seemed terribly aware of her hand on his arm, so Libby let it slide down to her side.

"Cheyenne visits me a couple of times a week. Often Jackson comes with her."

Nodding, Libby wasn't yet ready to let him go. "You said that when she was born, you and Cheyenne were brought back to Crooked Arrow. But you never said what it was like for you during your early years in Prosperino. Having to leave the reservation when you were so young must have been hard for you."

His mouth drew into a taut line and his dark eyes went flat as he shut down on her.

"You wouldn't find my story an interesting one. Believe me."

Just as she was about to protest, he continued, "But I do have something to tell you."

He gazed out the kitchen window, and she realized suddenly that the sun had risen, that its rays warmed the side of her face.

"While I was out there this morning—" with a slight lift of his chin he indicated the yard beyond the clear glass pane "—I decided it was time to come clean."

"Come clean about what?" She'd been curious about his youth and thought that discovering more about his childhood, his upbringing, might give her some insight into the vast complexities of who he was.

She'd noticed that he had what could almost be described as a chip on his shoulder when it came to figures of authority. Especially when those authority figures were male and their skin was white.

Libby remembered the harshness of his tone when he spoke of the anti-Native American sentiment that ran rampant through the all-Caucasian board of directors at Springer, Inc. Of the board, only her father, a man who did what he could to help the local Mokee-kittuun, had been spared Rafe's verbal wrath. She'd noticed how he'd looked at the guards at the jailhouse. And he'd acted a bit prickly around Sergeant Lummus at the hospital emergency room, as well.

She suspected Rafe's attitude stemmed from his years living under Curtis James's roof. Prosperino was a small town. And although she hadn't been able to bring herself to reveal this information to Rafe, Libby knew Curtis James had carried around the label of town drunk.

"I didn't feel comfortable admitting this before now," he said. "But I arrived on your doorstep with...um..."

One of his sun-kissed shoulders lifted in a shrug.

"Well, I guess you could say I have a theory about the case."

Libby didn't bother to conceal her surprise. "You know who's behind the DMBE contamination?"

"Not who," he told her. "Only why."

"You should have said something."

He had issues with trust. Hadn't she just surmised that those issues stemmed from his childhood upbringing? However, she'd thought his lack of trust was focused on those who, for one reason or another, made him experience a feeling of powerlessness. But now she was recognizing that his trust issues ran deeper than she first thought. He hadn't been able to confide in her his thoughts and opinions regarding her father's case. Well, he hadn't until now.

She'd love if he would open his heart to her, reveal his reasons for not feeling secure enough with her to divulge his theories. But he'd already shut her out once this morning. So digging into his psyche would have to wait. Right now she'd have to be content talking about the case.

"Why, Rafe? What do you think is motivating the person who's responsible for the contamination?"

The dark orbs of his pupils were so intense that Libby felt a shiver skitter down her spine.

"The land. They want the land."

"What land?"

Unwittingly, Rafe reached up and smoothed his palm across his chest. "Several months ago your father met with the Mokee-kittuun Elders. He explained that Springer was in need of land to expand their operation. He asked the Elders if the people would be willing to sell or even lease a strip of land for this expansion effort.''

He paused, leaned his hip against the counter. ''The Elders didn't even consider the idea before they turned him down. Crooked Arrow isn't a large reservation. The land is limited. The Elders wouldn't think of selling off a square inch of it, let alone a large strip.''

His gaze softened. ''Most men would have reacted to the rejection in anger and frustration. But not David. Your father noticed the living conditions of many of the families on the rez. He offered to have Springer drill a new well as a means to help us and he made it happen.''

She remembered the well construction site she'd seen on the way to Rafe's home. Her heart warmed to think that her father was responsible. He was a compassionate man and that made Libby proud.

''But I don't understand what your story has to do with the contamination.''

''I believe that someone at Springer was determined to have the land. Even after David's request was denied. I believe that some evil-minded person meant to poison the land. Make it useless for living on, working on. I think this person deliberately dumped the DMBE so that the land would be worthless and the Elders would then sell to Springer.''

Rafe's theory was so horrible it made Libby sick to her stomach.

Almost to herself, she said, ''I had so hoped we'd find that the contamination was an accident. I still hope that's the case.''

''The executive board wouldn't have fired your father,'' Rafe said, ''wouldn't be doing all it can to crucify him, if that were so.''

She tucked her bottom lip between her teeth, realizing in her heart that he made a convincing argument.

Her mind began churning over all that he'd said. "But the premise you pose has a hole in it. A big one. If someone meant to contaminate the water of Crooked Arrow, how come no one from the reservation has become sick? The DMBE showed up in Hopechest's water, and a small amount has been detected in the town water."

"It has to do with the aquifer flow."

He sighed, his face taking on a curious masked expression.

"I'm a rancher, Libby. My livelihood depends on the land, the water, the very air. My animals need plenty of fresh water to drink. Fresh green grass to eat. I know the land." He looked away for a moment, then leveled his eyes on her once again. "The rez land wasn't contaminated, but it *was* the target. You'll have to trust me on this."

Trust him? Why should she trust him? He hadn't trusted her with all this information before now.

But suddenly the tension in her neck and shoulders relaxed. She did trust him. She didn't have a clue how he knew what he knew; she was only certain that she had faith in his knowledge.

"We should tell someone about this."

Rafe only shook his head. "It looks bad for David. He came to Crooked Arrow to ask for land. His request was denied…."

She finished for him. "And now the land's been contaminated and Springer is helping the authorities to convict my father for the crime." Her exhalation was soulful. "You're right. Oh, Rafe, it looks very bad."

Nine

"**O**kay, that's it."

At the sound of Libby's voice, Rafe looked up from the papers he was reading. She tossed a pen onto the table.

"I'm tired, I'm starved and if I don't get out into the fresh air soon, I think I'm going to mummify."

He looked at the clock, his eyes widening in surprise. "I can't believe we worked through dinner. No wonder you're starved. It's late."

They had plowed through another box of evidence. They had found some office memorandums from Springer that mentioned the meeting David had had with the Mokee-kittuun Elders. The inter-office notes had depressed Libby as she had begun to understand that the lawyers who meant to prosecute her father really might have a plausible case to present. Rafe had been determined to keep reading through the evidence until they found something—*anything*—that pointed to David's innocence. So far, however, that hadn't happened.

"You know," Libby told him, "I never did get my burger from Jake's. I wrecked my car nearly a week ago, but I never got my sirloin burger. I say we hop in the car, buy a couple of burgers with the works and drive around while we eat. Let's let the wind blow through our hair a bit. We just might benefit from having the cobwebs puffed from our brains. What do you say?"

Rafe chuckled. "I don't mind going out to eat. But, Libby, if you haven't noticed, it's chilly."

Lord, but she was beautiful when she laughed. Her teeth gleamed, her whole face lit up.

"Okay, okay. So we keep the windows up. And if you're nice to me—" she grinned at him "—I'll even let you turn on the heater."

The magic that constantly hovered between them glittered and sparkled like so many stars in a velvet night sky.

"You've got a deal."

The night was nippy and thick with fog. Perfectly normal weather for March in northern California when half the annual precipitation fell. This close to the ocean, snow was almost unheard of. So residents just lived with the cold misty rain and viscous fog that came with winter.

"Isn't it a beautiful night?" Libby turned onto the main road connecting Crooked Arrow and Prosperino.

Rafe had to laugh. "Woman, you *have* been cooped up in the house too long."

It wasn't long before the tires of Libby's rental car crunched over the gravel-covered parking lot of Jake's. The rental car agency had hesitated about handing the keys of a replacement after what had happened to the other auto, but in the end they relented. She pulled the car to a halt among the rows of parked autos in the ill-lit lot.

"I'll go in," he told her.

"No way. You've been feeding me for days. Dinner's on me tonight." She cut the engine and took the keys from the ignition. "Sit tight. I'll be right back."

He watched her go inside and then let his back muscles melt against the seat back. Another car arrived, and three people, laughing and joking, made their way into the small bar and grill. Judging from the look of the full lot, Rafe decided he was in for a wait. But surprisingly Libby exited the building not long after, and he easily identified her even in the fog as the distorted light shining from over the front door of Jake's made her wild array of curls glow a soft copper.

"That was quick," he murmured to himself.

Glancing down between the seat and the door, he wrestled with the buckle of the seat belt that had become twisted when he'd disconnected it. He pulled the belt across his chest and fastened it with a *click*.

Her scream ripped through the night, freezing the blood in his veins. She wrestled with someone in the murky haze just beyond the muted light thrown by the fixture above the door. Adrenaline pumped through Rafe's body. Precious seconds seemed to lumber by as he fumbled with the clasp of the seat belt. He cursed silently. Finally, the latch released and he shoved open the passenger side door, a thought floating somewhere in the back of his brain that he'd probably chipped the paint of the neighboring car.

"Libby!"

He moved toward the building, scanning the lot. He heard the scuffling of shoes on gravel, but wasn't able to pinpoint her exact location.

"F-fire, fire, *f-fire!*"

Another scream, more scuffling, and Rafe sprinted forward, darting between the cars, following the sound of Libby's voice, the sound of shoes on loose stone. The back of the dark cloaked figure was to him, and clamping his hands on the man's shoulders, Rafe twisted with all his might. The man turned, sweeping his arm wide. Steel glinted dully in the mist and Rafe instinctively jerked back. But the move was not fast enough. Pain burned in his side.

With one hand still on Libby, the man shoved her to the ground and raced away between the cars, disappearing behind the building.

"You okay?" He helped her to her feet.

"Y-yes," she told him. "M-my knees are like j-jelly, though. I was scared to death. I was sure that creep was going to run off with my purse."

All he wanted to do was hold her against his chest, give thanks to The Great One that she was safe. Instead, he said, "Go inside and call the police. I'm going after him."

She pinched his sleeve. "N-n-no!" Then looked down the length of him. Her eyes widened. She lifted her gaze to his. "You're hurt."

"I didn't realize he had a knife," Rafe murmured, "until it was too late." He looked in the direction the man disappeared. "I'm going after him, Libby."

"You are n-not."

Her tone was emphatic, her grip on his jacket tightening.

"W-we're going to the hospital."

"Libby, the guy tried to hurt you. He's getting away."

She inhaled deeply and closed her eyes, seeming to

shut out everything for a moment or two. Rafe perceived that she was attempting to calm herself.

"Let him get away," she finally said. Then using both hands, she parted the facings of his jacket. "I want to know how badly you're hurt."

She enunciated every word carefully and the oddness of it should have dawned on him. But the concern in her voice touched his heart. And the oh-so-gentle manner in which she took hold of the fabric made him give up on the idea of catching her attacker.

She attempted to tug the ruined T-shirt from the waistband of his jeans.

He winced.

"I'm sorry, Rafe." Bending down, she snatched up her purse. "Come on. Let's get to the E.R."

When he balked, her frowning gaze met his.

"I'm not going to the hospital. I have plenty of bandages and salves at home."

"But you haven't even seen the cut. It might need stitches."

"If that's the case, then I'll see a doctor on the rez."

"Oh."

She seemed at a loss for words, which he found amazing and amusing.

They started toward Libby's car.

"So," he began lightly, "what was that 'fire, fire' business all about?"

"The firm I work for in San Francisco invited a speaker to come in and talk about self-defense," she told him. "The man said that when most people hear someone scream for help, they turn their heads, not wanting to get involved. But if they hear the word fire, then their first thought is, 'Hey, I might be in danger here.' So, they get up and see what the commotion is all about."

"I see." Suddenly he felt giddy. He suspected the silliness churning in his gut was a result of the huge relief he felt knowing that Libby was safe and sound.

Evidently she saw the humor glittering in his eyes, and she glared. "If you weren't hurt right now, I'd slug you for laughing at me. Now get in the car before I leave you standing here."

"But I'm not laugh—"

Her glare had him saluting.

"Yes, ma'am. Whatever you say, ma'am." Pulling open the car door, he gingerly slid into the passenger seat.

The air seemed…strange. Charged. *Electrified.*

During the drive back to Rafe's house, the atmosphere between them had thickened. The humming current had grown stronger…more potent with each passing moment.

Libby couldn't say if it was the ever-present attraction that caused this amazing and startling phenomenon or the aftermath of the acute threat they had faced together.

Probably both, she surmised.

The bathroom was small, and Libby's hip was pressed against the porcelain counter while she bent over to clean and dress Rafe's cut. The wound had turned out to be quite superficial, a long, angry-looking scratch. But it had bled enough to stain his T-shirt. So Libby washed the area with soap and water, and used a fresh towel to pat his skin dry.

His stomach was taut, the muscles beneath the bronzed skin hard and rippled. She'd dreamed about running her fingers over the hills and valleys of the corded sinew so many times since she'd met this man. So many times. In the deepest hours of the night. And in the wide-awake hours of the day.

Her hands trembled as she smeared an antibiotic cream

over the cut. Then she took the bandage he offered and gently pressed it into place.

He sucked in his breath.

"Sorry," she murmured.

"Stings a bit, is all."

It was then that she made her fatal error. Tipping up her chin, she lifted her gaze to his.

There was concentrated power in his intense mahogany eyes. Power that held her captive. Power that mesmerized her. Power she found fascinating. Enthralling.

The expression on his face told her in no uncertain terms that he was relieved and more than a little thankful that nothing bad had happened to her in that dark parking lot tonight.

But how could anything bad have happened to her? With Rafe to protect her, she was safe. Completely safe. *Safe.*

The word echoed through her head. She hadn't felt safe with a man in a very long time. Libby felt her whole body relax.

The attraction that had throbbed between them from the very start, that had haunted the two of them like some ghostly wraith, had been nearly unbearable, impossible to deny. But she'd had very good reasons for ignoring the feelings and desires that Rafe stirred in her. And she'd felt that she'd done an excellent job of discounting what was between them.

Until this moment.

What would it hurt to trace her fingers along his firm stomach? Why should she continue to deny herself—and him—the pleasure that awaited them both?

Rafe was an honorable man. A man she could trust. He'd proved that over and over. He'd probably saved her life tonight. She hadn't known the purse snatcher had wielded a knife when she'd fought him. That thieving creep could very well have used that knife on her had Rafe not come to her rescue so quickly, if he hadn't been so willing to put himself between her and the danger she'd faced.

He'd stood by her side since she'd arrived in Prosperino.

And he'd wanted her all that time. Just as she'd wanted him.

She knew it. And she knew he knew it.

His abdomen was warm under her fingertips, the muscle rock-hard. He sucked in his breath, and for a split second, she panicked, thinking that she'd hurt him. But she read surprise in his handsome, hawklike features, and her mouth tightened with a smile. She liked the idea that she could shock him. Liked it very much, indeed.

Boldly, she let her eyes rove down his torso. Slowly. An open invitation.

She stopped when her gaze lit on his belly button. For some reason, she found the sight of it more sexy than she could stand.

Her heartbeat thrummed. Her blood raced.

Libby leaned in and kissed the smooth skin just above it. He smelled luscious. Woodsy, like warm cedar. Parting her lips, she tasted him, dragging a languorous tongue over his velvet flesh. Hearing him inhale a long, ragged breath, she smiled against his skin, feeling triumphant.

With nimble fingers, she was able to unfasten the buckle of his belt, but then his quelling hands covered hers. He cradled her face, guiding her away from his delicious body. She straightened her spine then, tipped up her chin so she was standing face to face with him.

"Do you know what you're doing?"

His voice resonated with emotion so profound, so soul-shattering that it nearly stole her breath away.

She opened her mouth to speak, but she was so affected by him, by what was happening between them, that no words would flow forth. Finally, determined to make him see that she was lucid, fully conscious of the moment, she forced herself to whisper, ''I know exactly what I'm doing.''

Sure of what she wanted, she flashed her eyes at him, flirtatious and saucy. ''I also know exactly what we're about to do.''

His hesitation lasted but one heartbeat, then his mouth crushed down on hers.

His kiss was rough, brutal. Just what her pent-up desire had been yearning for for oh-so long.

His teeth raked her lips, his tongue plunged deeply into the soft recesses of her mouth. And she opened herself to his forceful plundering, her pulse thumping, her passions igniting.

He kissed her cheek, her jaw, her neck, and she tilted her head, offering him the full length of her throat for the taking. And take he did. Libby felt ravaged. She felt wonderful. She felt *delirious*.

Desire coursed through her body like molten magma. She drove her fingers into his hair, combing through the length of it, reveling in the cool, silky texture that was so at odds with the scorch of his mouth against her skin.

Impatiently, Rafe tugged at her top, tugged it up over her bra, up over her head, and it tumbled to the tiled floor of the bathroom.

With his hands, his mouth, his tongue, he made his tender attack on her breasts, and she felt she would die from the sheer glory of the assault. Her nipples tightened into hard buds under his fingertips and tongue. He kissed and tasted and touched until she was gasping for breath.

She kissed the hardness of his biceps, the smooth roundness of his shoulder, the corded curve of his neck. She pinched the lobe of his ear between her front teeth. Curling her fingers, she ran her nails lightly up his chest, and she was rewarded by his groan.

The panting and moaning they emitted only inflamed the fervent rage that had caught them up, swept them away.

She kissed him full on the mouth. Blindly, her eager fingers reached for and found the metal fastener of his jeans. The zipper glided down, and she broke the kiss in order to tug the denim fabric over his hips and thighs. He stepped out of the pants, kicking them aside as if they had been a hindrance for longer than he could bear.

They moved into the hallway, kissing, touching, tasting, rubbing, kneading, aching, wanting, *craving*. Their breathing had become stentorian to her ears. Deafening. Exciting.

He tugged her trousers down over her hips and she walked out of them, leaving them where they lay.

The sleek curtain of his hair fell across the full length of her arm when he reached behind her to unclasp her bra. The lacy fabric was tossed aside.

They reached the threshold of his bedroom and he removed her panties, his strong hands sliding down the length of her legs. She stood breathless as his dark, feverish gaze made a slow, thorough scan of her nakedness. Rather than feeling shy and vulnerable, she marveled at how secure he made her feel.

Her heart pounded. Her throat went dry. Oh, how she wanted this man, this moment.

Almost as if reading her thoughts, he asked, "You're sure?"

She didn't hesitate. "I've never been more sure of anything in my life."

He picked her up then and carried her to his bed. The mattress was soft, enveloping, and she reclined, letting her eyes feast on the sight of his nearly nude body. The fabric of his briefs and the small, square bandage on his ribs were both stark white against his golden skin. Her gaze darted to his briefs, and seeming to understand her silent wish, he reached down and removed the last article of his clothing.

He was gorgeous. His body was heavenly. Tall. Strong. Beautiful.

The mattress depressed under his weight, and Libby closed her eyes and took great pleasure in the feel of his fingers lightly skimming up the full length of her. Over ankle, shin bone, knee and thigh. Then he tarried, lightly teasing her triangle of springy hair. Libby felt herself grow moist, need pulsing deep inside. But then his fingertips resumed their journey up her body, over her belly and breasts and neck, jaw and cheek and temple. There his roving stopped and he stretched out beside her, his handsome face looming above hers.

The fever pitch had calmed, his kiss was softer now, gentler, more giving, and she drank in the heat of him, the smell of him, the feel of his mouth, the taste of his tongue. His hands cupped her face. His hair tickled her skin with every move he made. His warm breath was on her neck. His fingers were in her hair.

She'd been stirred by his fervent attack just a moment ago, had enjoyed snatching and taking right along with him. But this slow, languid lovemaking was just as wonderful, just as arousing.

Her need was building. Pulsing, urging, calling.

Letting her fingers slide up his arms, over his shoulders, she whispered his name, and knew that the tremor in her tone conveyed all the yearning she suffered. His kiss was deep, one hand smoothing down her abdomen, finding and gently exploring the most sensitive part of her. When the pad of his fingertip grazed what to her at that instant was the very center of her being, she whimpered against his mouth and lifted her hips toward his touch. Her knees seemed to part of their own accord. He eased himself on top of her, resting the bulk of his weight on his elbows, his breathing seeming to come in great and jagged gulps.

He guided himself into her, his movements unhurried, deliberate, and she thought she'd die from the waiting. When he filled her, he gazed down into her face. The dark mass of his shining hair was like a drape that hid them from the outside world. All that existed was the two of them—and the desire that vibrated and hummed and sang.

"Libby."

She found the sound of his voice overwhelming, and she reached up and took his face between her hands.

"Kiss me." The desperation in her tone was undeniable, and even that inflamed her. She guided him down, down, until their lips met.

His hips ground slowly against hers, and she lifted herself up to meet him. Her hands found his shoulders and she gripped them, her fingertips digging deep. The pulsing at her very center escalated, expanded, until the scope of it surrounded—*became*—her total consciousness.

Still, Rafe took her higher.

Emotions spiraled and tipped and careened, and she gasped when a thunderous explosion of feeling ended with a tumbling and rolling, glittering like colorful gems that had been tossed, helter-skelter, onto black velvet.

Libby lay there panting, smiling up into his face. But she could tell by the look in his eyes, by the hard length of him between her legs, that he hadn't reached orgasm. Excitement skittered in her stomach. Lifting one hip, she nudged at him, and they rolled together as one.

His hair pooled on the sheets, hers was wild about them. She splayed her hands on his chest, kissed the tip of his nose. And with tiny, lolling movements of her hips, she rode him. Drowsily. Lazily.

Rafe closed his eyes, let his arms relax in total enjoyment. This was his time, and evidently he meant to take full advantage of it.

But as she moved on him, her own need resurged. Her breath quickened. Her blood raced. And before she realized, her eyelids slid shut and she was once again focused only on the desire thudding through her. Again, she climaxed with what felt like a delirious rumble.

Her skin felt damp and she reached up to comb her hair out of her face.

How selfish could she be? She'd meant to pleasure him as he had her. However, she'd gotten caught up in the feel of him, in the passion he stirred in her.

But when she looked down at Rafe, there was no doubt whatsoever that his need had been satiated.

When he finally opened his eyes and gazed up into her face, she said, "Thanks for rescuing me at Jake's tonight. I was scared half to death."

Rafe smoothed his hands over her thighs. "If this is how you're going to thank me, I'll fight off any man who comes within a mile of you."

She chuckled, then she drew a small circle around his

russet nipple. "This had nothing to do with your keeping that creep from stealing my purse."

His brows raised. "You don't really believe that's what he was after, do you? That man meant to hurt you."

"Oh, Rafe," she said. "Don't start with that again. We haven't had any trouble for days. We weren't followed when we left here. How could anyone know we'd show up at Jake's?"

"It was in the paper. I read it."

"What are you talking about?"

"After you'd been run off the road, you told the reporter you'd been on your way to Jake's. Don't you remember? You even said that Jake's had the best burgers in town."

"Oh, that article about my accident was lucky to have received two inches of column space." Her head rested on his bare chest. "I think you're wrong. I think someone was looking for some quick cash, and he thought he'd take some of mine." She grinned. "Little did he know that I travel with my very own bodyguard."

But he was obviously unconvinced.

She remained straddling him, the two of them most intimately connected. She reached out and traced down the length of his nose, over his top lip. He opened his mouth, took her fingertip between his teeth, his tongue skating the soft pad. Then he sucked gently. And Libby felt her pulse quicken.

Without warning, he trailed the fingers of both his hands up over her hips and waist. She squirmed off him, laughing as she tumbled onto the mattress.

"You're ticklish."

He seemed delighted to have found a weakness in her. His dark eyes gleamed as he rose onto all fours. He looked the predator. Fierce as a wolf. Hungry as one, too.

And Libby was giddy knowing she was the prey in his sights.

"Don't you dare," she warned, wriggling toward the head of the bed.

She grabbed a pillow, trying to fend him off, but it proved a flimsy shield. He seized it with quick hands, tossed it aside.

"Rafe." Her continued retreat only seemed to encourage him. The farther back she inched, the closer he came. *"Rafe."*

Finally, he grabbed her ankle, his long, tapering fingers gentle but persistent. He pulled and she found herself being dragged back to the center of the mattress. She laughed, but did not fight him. In the blink of an eye, she was pinned beneath him.

Pinned by his body. And by his burning brown eyes.

She was just where she wanted to be.

"You're a beautiful woman," he said. "And I think I've wanted you my whole life."

He kissed her, then. Long. Resolute. Arduous.

Healing.

And Libby felt the delicious heated spirals beginning all over again.

Ten

Libby felt the warm, buttery sunlight on her body even before she was fully awake. She stretched like a lazy cat and then curled over onto her side. Sensing she was alone in Rafe's bed, she reached over and pulled his pillow to her and hugged it.

Oh, but she had never experienced the kind of love-making Rafe had showered on her last night. He'd taken her to the very pinnacle, again and again, until she'd been weak and breathless. And she had loved every moment of it.

After her experience in the past, she'd never thought she could trust enough to fall in love again. But she had.

Rafe, she realized, was the man of her dreams. The love of her life. And she wanted to be with him forever and a day.

She chuckled. That sounded so silly. So schoolgirlish. But that was exactly how she felt.

Bounding out of Rafe's bed, she hurried to her room, picking up the clothes they had so thoughtlessly discarded the night before. Her face heated, thinking that he'd had to walk past her now wrinkled trousers, her crumpled panties, her top and bra on his way to the kitchen this morning.

After tossing the clothing on the perfectly made bed in the guest room, she shoved her legs into a fresh pair of panties and jeans and then tugged on a white cotton shirt. She couldn't wait to see Rafe this morning. To wish him a good morning. To thank him for the wonderment he'd shown her in the night. To express her gratitude for the pleasure he'd given. To tell him all that was in her heart. To show him all the things she felt. And finally, she meant to somehow articulate her appreciation that he'd healed her wounded soul.

Because of him, she was able to love again. That was the most important piece of information she needed to relay. She poured two cups of coffee and then went out the back door to search for him.

The Appaloosa he groomed was white, its black spots standing out sharply in contrast. It was a stately animal, and it nickered and nodded its head at her appearance.

"Whoa, boy," Rafe crooned softly. "It's okay."

He never stopped stroking the brush over the horse's coat.

Although it was hard to tamp down the thrill of seeing Rafe, she kept her tone quiet, her body movements conservative, so as not to startle the animals nearby when she said, "Morning."

He tossed her a quick glance over his shoulder, and when her gaze connected with his, her nipples budded to life beneath the thin cotton fabric of her top. It never entered her head to feel self-conscious of her physical reaction to him.

Rafe ran the brush over the Appaloosa's mane, then he led the animal to its pen and hung a leather feeding bag within its reach.

"I brought you some coffee," she told him.

Still, he remained silent. It was only when he turned to face her fully that she knew that something was terribly wrong.

Damn! Why did she have to be so exquisite? Why did her hair have to glow like liquid fire? Why did her skin have to be so creamy? Her eyes so sparkling and clear? Why did her breasts have to be so utterly perfect? Why did her nipples have to draw up into such tantalizing buds right before his very eyes? Why did her legs have to be so long and shapely? Why did she have to have such interesting opinions? Why was her wit so quick? Why did she have to be so caring?

Why did she have to be so…so…*appealing?*

Damn it all to hell! Why did his flesh have to be so weak?

He'd promised to keep his hands to himself. No matter how much he might have burned to touch her, he'd silently vowed he wouldn't.

It was a vow he'd broken.

And he'd go to his grave being sorry for that.

But, sorry excuse for a man that he was, he'd forever cherish the memories of the night he'd held her in his arms. The night they'd made sweet love until the both of them had moaned with pure pleasure.

His eyes narrowed. He had to remain focused. He had to do what was right.

Libby was too good for the likes of him. It would be

completely unfair to encumber her with such a heavy burden. His twisted childhood had left him emotionally crippled. One night of passion didn't change that fact. She should not have to deal with his problems, or the everyday burden he'd bring simply by being who he was.

She was worthy of only the best of men. She deserved normalcy. No, she deserved love and romance in its highest form.

Libby deserved happily ever after.

He was not the man to give her that. His emotions were maimed and mangled beyond recognition.

Sometimes, in the deepest hours of the night, thoughts of Curtis James and the brutal treatment he'd doled out would fill Rafe with such rage that he was unable to keep still. Half insane with anger and bitterness, he'd saddle one of his horses and ride hard into the darkness, hoping, praying for some kind of release.

He never wanted Libby to see him lose control like that. She should not have to pay for the dysfunctional upbringing he'd suffered. He would not allow that to happen.

Doing the right thing by her was all that was in his mind.

He went to her, took the coffee from her, keeping his face impassive. Then he paced to the door of the outbuilding and flung the steaming brown liquid to the ground.

When he turned back to face her, she looked as if he'd slapped her in the face. He had to ignore that. He simply had to disregard her reaction to what he was about to say.

She'd be hurt. But he must remain unaffected and tell her the truth, nonetheless.

"I don't want any coffee."

A tiny crease appeared between her eyes. He wanted

nothing more than to go to her, to smooth away her frown with a gentle touch. But he couldn't.

"And you need to know," he continued, "last night was a mistake. A terrible mistake that can't happen again."

He enunciated the word *mistake* both times he said it, and she flinched with each utterance. His words were wounding her, he knew. And it killed him. It wasn't his intention to be cruel. Just honest. She needed to understand his thoughts in no uncertain terms. All of this was for her own good.

Her face was pale as porcelain. He'd derailed her with his attitude. She'd come out here anticipating everything would be rosy, expecting the morning to be filled with sunshine and kisses, but what she got was flat-out rejection.

Rafe hoped she wouldn't cry. He seriously doubted he could stand firm in the face of her tears.

When he saw her gaze light with ire, he was relieved. Anger. Now that was something he could handle.

"Men are such big, fat jerks."

Her tone was low, ominous, and for a moment he feared she might throw a cup at him. He kept a careful eye on her, ready to dodge if the need arose. But she set it down, balancing it on top of one of the stall posts.

"You and Stephen are two peas in a pod."

What was she talking about? *Who* was she talking about?

She turned and looked out the door. "But maybe it's me. Maybe the problem doesn't lie with the men, but with the stupid woman who trusts them. And that stupid woman is me!"

When she lifted her gaze to his, he was nearly knocked back a step by the fury registered in her aquamarine eyes.

"I trusted you," she said. "Just like I trusted him. I gave him everything I had to give. I made him my whole world."

Rafe felt his throat close up. He didn't want to hear this. But that didn't stop her.

"I fell desperately in love with a man who *I thought* wanted to spend the rest of his life with me. But there were a few things he forgot to tell me about. Like a wife and a couple of kids. When I found out about his family, I confronted him. And—"

Her voice broke then; however, she paused to take a deep breath and evidently to rein in her emotions.

"And you know what he did?" she continued, her tone once again resilient. "He laughed. Right in my face. I've never been more humiliated in my life. He said I was nothing more to him than a toy. A sexual plaything he'd never planned to keep around for very long."

She seethed. "I vowed back then that I'd never allow myself to be used again. Yet here I stand, feeling just as exploited and abused and taken advantage of as I did back then." She glared at him. "I just hope this little fling was fun for you. I just hope it was."

Libby turned then and raced toward the house, leaving Rafe standing there not knowing what the hell to think.

The clothes she'd stuffed into her suitcase would be wrinkled beyond repair. But Libby didn't care. All she wanted was to get out of Rafe's house, to get away from that insufferable man.

She could not believe she'd let down her defenses. She'd let him into her heart. She'd freely offered him the gift of her body. To think that she'd awoken this morning actually believing he'd healed her. The very idea made her stomach solidify into a granite-hard mass. She couldn't believe she'd actually allowed herself to think that she might be in love with the man.

You *are* in love with the man.

The thought soughed through her brain like a cool breeze, but it did nothing to calm her spirit.

"No." The spoken word reverberated off the walls of the bedroom. "I'm not. I won't let myself love him."

You think you can stop what you feel? What is...*is*. You have no control over it. There's no changing reality.

What she'd felt for Stephen all those years ago in law school was a single, tiny drop in an overflowing rain barrel compared to what she felt for Rafe James. There was no disputing that fact. No denying it.

There was no changing reality.

The revelation depressed her.

"Well, then," she said aloud, "that's just all the more reason for me to get the hell out of here."

"That's not a good idea."

Gasping, she whirled toward the door, toward the sound of Rafe's voice.

"You're not going anywhere."

Her chin tipped up stubbornly. "Your days of telling me what I will and won't do are over."

"Look, Libby, I understand why you're angry. You're furious with me. And you've got every right to be. But don't let your anger make you do something impulsive."

"Oh, I think it's safe to say that I've used up all my impulsive chips in this game we've been playing. I used them up last night, as a matter of fact. Every single one of them." She narrowed her gaze on him when she spoke the final sentence.

At least he had sense enough to grimace.

She closed the lid of the case and locked the latches with two sharp snaps.

"We can still work together, Libby," he said. "What happened between us shouldn't hinder our working relationship."

Her fingers tightened on the handle of the case and she lifted it off the bed.

He insisted, "There's too much for you to do all alone."

When she tried to pass him, he took her arm. His touch felt like the bare wires of an electric cord, stinging hot, but she'd die before she cringed from him.

"Libby—"

His tone was emphatic, and her eyes were drawn to his face as if he were emitting some strange kind of magnetic current she was unable to resist.

"—it isn't safe for you to leave here."

"Give it up, Rafe! No one believes that but you. The police agree with me that some inexperienced kid ran me off the road in the rain. And that man wanted my money last night not my life.

The muscle in his jaw tensed.

"You're wrong about my being in danger. Dead wrong."

Her chest was heaving with a flurry of emotion. She felt humiliated that she'd given herself to Rafe and then he'd practically kicked her aside. She felt ashamed of herself for having lowered her guard after she'd promised herself she wouldn't. And she felt hurt. Oh, how her soul burned with hurt.

"But what if I'm dead right? What if you go out there and get yourself killed? Who will be David's champion then, Libby? Who will save him then?"

His questions seemed to hit her like solid punches to the chin, the stomach, the jaw. When he finished speaking, she was trembling. Surely, her knees wouldn't hold her weight for much longer.

"We can get over this," he continued, his tone, his whole body stance, cajoling. Then his spine straightened. "In the grand scheme of things, what happened between us is a small bump in the road. We can roll over it, get beyond it and still work as a team. We need each other, Libby. And more than anything else, David needs us. Working together as a team."

Feeling pathetically confused, Libby stood there, silent. She didn't know whom she was more furious with—Rafe, for callously using her, or herself, for knocking down the wall she'd built around her heart and inviting the man in.

We need each other, Libby. And more than anything else, David needs us.

She might be an idiot where affairs of the heart were concerned, but she took the job of defending her father seriously. And she was determined to see him a free man once again. Nothing would keep her from that goal. Not even her own stupidity over her feelings for Rafe, over having trusted him with her heart when he didn't deserve that trust, nor over having been used and humiliated once again by a man.

Nothing mattered more than saving her father. Nothing.

Although she hated to admit it, she had to consider that small percentage of a chance that Rafe might be right about her safety.

She was the only family her father had left. He loved her. And he'd want her to play it smart. He certainly wouldn't want her taking chances—Libby glared at Rafe—no matter how much she might want to.

With a sigh that was laced with both irritation and resignation, she set down the suitcase.

Eleven

"**L**ooks like something big is happening."

Although Libby agreed with Rafe's comment, she remained silent. A horde of people crowded the front of the courthouse, spilling from the steps to the sidewalk, even into the street. The scene looked more like a cheap carnival sideshow than the main thoroughfare of a small town.

Her nerves danced a jig as she wondered what had caused all this ruckus.

"You want me to come inside with you?" he asked. "See you through this crowd safely?"

Tensions between herself and Rafe had been tightrope taut ever since their night of passion. She loved the man, yes. But feeling betrayed by him and knowing he wanted nothing to do with her, she was also angry as hell at him.

"No thank you." Her voice felt and sounded constricted. "You can pick me up here in a few hours."

She got out of his truck, but before she had a chance to shut the door, the prosecuting attorney approached her.

The man held out a fat manila envelope. "Courier tried to deliver this to you last night and couldn't find you."

Something in his tone had Libby feeling as if he was blaming her for that. "I left word with the court clerk about where I was staying."

He shrugged. "It was after hours. Couldn't reach the clerk. By the way, I told the judge we'd be ready to start jury selection in a couple of days. As soon as I have time to review this new evidence. Judge has postponed all further arguments until everyone gets a chance to see this."

His slow smile left her feeling as if a snake had just slithered across her skin.

"I think you'll find it very interesting."

He walked away from her, and she only had time to toss the envelope onto the front seat of Rafe's truck before she was besieged by a group of reporters.

"In light of this new evidence," one man fairly shouted at her, "can you tell us if your father is ready to confess?"

Apprehension had Libby's skin feeling flushed. "I haven't had time to review this new evidence you're talking about, so I have no comment at this time."

"We were told it looks like a diary," another reporter spoke up.

One woman added, "Computer generated is what they said."

Frustrated, Libby murmured under her breath. "*They* shouldn't have said anything."

"Apparently, this thing's got David Corbett's name stamped all over it," another reporter shouted.

Libby wanted to tell him she was only two feet from him and that there was nothing wrong with her hearing.

Instead, she stated, "This is obviously some kind of sabotage. Our experts will prove that."

"Technological sabotage." A female journalist scribbled as she spoke. "Sounds intriguing. You really think you can prove it?"

"I *know* I can." She backed her way, inch by inch, into the cab of the truck, one knee up on the seat, her head ducked low. "I have no further comments at this time." She shut the door.

"Looks like I have the day free." She swiveled around until she was sitting on the seat properly. "Also sounds like we're going to need it."

Rafe had opened the envelope and was scanning the documents. "It does look like a diary. Or a journal. Just like they said. Computer generated, too. And David's name is on each page."

He handed the packet over to her and then put the truck into gear. "You have access to computer experts?" he asked, darting a look at traffic before pulling onto the roadway.

"Not yet."

"Libby."

The admonition in his tone had her wishing she could disappear into thin air.

"You shouldn't be making rash statements like that to the press. You know that's going to show up in the papers this afternoon."

She shrugged. "By then maybe we'll have hired some experts."

This new evidence contained pages and pages of text. Libby leafed through it. She couldn't quite believe what she was seeing.

"Bad. This is bad," she muttered to herself.

The electronic journal, its entries dated every few days,

was written by someone who was very unhappy with Springer, Inc., someone who wanted to damage the oil company's reputation. And Rafe was right. Her father's name was on each and every post.

"Let's go see Dad." She flipped through the pages. "He needs to see this. Maybe he can tell us where it came from and how his name got on it."

"You don't believe he had anything to do with this, do you?"

She sighed. "I don't know what to believe anymore." Stopping there would have been the thing to do. But doubts filled her like a flood tide rising in the Pacific. "I rushed to Prosperino thinking I could clear Dad's name like that." She snapped her fingers. "But now I'm not so sure. The odds seem to be stacking up against him." Her tone softened to a mere whisper. "Maybe Dad ought to have another lawyer. A big gun. Someone who's nationally known and has some clout behind his name."

Before she could say any more, Rafe pulled into the parking lot of the Prosperino jailhouse.

Rafe came out the front door of his house and offered Libby a glass of wine.

"Thanks," she said. But her gaze immediately returned to the far horizon.

Ever since she'd been handed that packet of evidence today at the courthouse, Libby had seemed more fragile than ever. The vulnerability she exuded ripped at his heart like the sharp talons of an eagle. It was all he could do not to reach out to her, reassure her.

David had denied any knowledge of the computerized diary the prosecution had found.

"I've filed the paperwork to get my hands on your company computer," Libby had told her father.

"That would be useless," David had told her. "Springer computers don't have individual hard drives. Any files and documents generated by computer are uploaded onto a private server. It's like a big mainframe hard drive, as I understand it. Everything is maintained and backed up regularly by the data department."

"So all someone had to do was create these documents with your name on them," Rafe had suggested, "and upload them onto the server."

Libby had brightened then. But David quickly dashed her hopes.

"I don't believe it's that easy," the older man had said. "The system is password protected."

"So someone stole your password."

Rafe had been taken aback by the tone of Libby's voice. Never had he heard her speak so sharply to her father.

After that, David had grown quiet. Rafe and Libby did decide to hire computer technicians to investigate the documents. They also resolved that, once they'd found their experts, they needed access to Springer's server.

Before they left the jail, David once again broached the subject of bargaining with the opposing council for a lesser charge. This had really flustered Libby, Rafe had seen that.

He'd known that David's suggestion had only been based on the fact that the deeper they dug into this mess, the more danger Libby was in. But David didn't want Libby to know that. So she was left silently thinking that her father had no faith in her knowledge of the law or in her ability as an attorney.

Rafe had sought her out, bringing an offering of wine, to somehow console her. To lift her spirits. However, doing so without revealing all the sordid details of the illegal chemical dumping, David's destroying of evidence and the breaking and entering of Libby's San Francisco apartment seemed impossible.

Sworn to secrecy regarding that whole incident, Rafe simply decided to do what he could.

"Everything is going to be okay," he told her. He eased himself down on the step beside her.

"I'm glad someone thinks so."

"Come on now, Libby. Things aren't that dire. You said you were going to call your firm in San Francisco. Did they give you the name of a computer firm that could help us out?"

"Actually, they did better than that," she said. "They're sending the best person they know. She'll be here tomorrow afternoon."

He smiled. "See there? Things are looking up."

Her gem-hued eyes found his.

I'm scared, was the unspoken message they conveyed. But Rafe knew she'd never admit her fear to him. Not after the way he'd hurt her.

He felt he deserved to suffer a horrendous punishment for what he'd done to her. He should never have given in to his body's desires. But he hadn't known about her past. He hadn't know that she'd been used, duped by a married man.

Well, any male who would betray his wife and his lover by being a conscious participant in infidelity really didn't deserve to be called a man.

Oh, heaven help him. Moonlight turned her skin to alabaster, her hair to shimmering copper. She was gorgeous, and sexy as hell. Being around this woman so much of the time had his hormones in a wild uproar. Need pulsed deep in his gut. But he'd ignore it. He had to.

She sipped her wine, and Rafe remembered how those luscious lips of hers had made his skin burn. She'd been an uninhibited lover. She'd driven him nearly mad with—

"What is that glow over there?" she asked.

He looked in the direction she pointed.

"A bonfire. The tribe is gathering. To celebrate the Spring Equinox."

She looked surprised. "You're not going?"

"Normally, I would. But…" He shrugged. "Well, I'm working. I can't be there and here, too. You need me to help read over those papers in there."

Interest sparked in her gaze. "Is this a religious ceremony?"

He paused, thinking over how he should explain the gathering taking place tonight.

"The Mokee-kittuun are more spiritual than religious," he told her. "Tonight the tribe will gather to sing praises to The Great Father. They'll ask his blessing on the spring planting. They'll pray for rain, for the crops and for a means to dilute the poison in Mother Earth."

She nodded, evidently understanding that he was speaking of the DMBE contamination. Then she smiled.

"Praising, praying. Sounds like a religious rite to me."

"They'll also spend time remembering the past. They'll tell folktales of great warriors, of times past." His voice lowered when he admitted, "Better times for our people." After a moment, he added, "There will be music and dancing and food."

"Then it's a party."

Excitement glittered in her deep aqua eyes, and his heart tripped in his chest. Never in his life had he seen a more stunningly beautiful woman.

After their intimate encounter, after their angry words,

that thought should have upset him. However, it didn't. In fact, the floating-on-air lightness churning inside him made him laugh.

"Yes, it's a party."

She studied her wine, then looked longingly at the glow of the bonfire on the horizon. He knew what was on her mind.

He asked, "Would you like to go see what it's all about?"

Her mouth drew into a wide smile. "Do you think anyone would mind?"

"Of course not," he told her. "But what about those boxes of evidence?"

"We really can't do a whole lot until the computer technician arrives tomorrow."

He smacked his knee with his flattened palm. "Then let's go celebrate."

Anticipation had Libby pacing the living room as she waited for Rafe. Yes, their relationship had been strained of late. And it probably would remain strained until they parted company when all this was over. But she really was interested in the Mokee-kittuun culture and traditions. Attending this celebration tonight would be an excellent way for her to experience them firsthand.

Rafe's heritage had gone a long way in carving out the man he was. Even though he'd rejected her and wounded her so, she was still eager to encounter even a small taste of American Indian tradition.

He'd gone to his room to "get dressed" for the evening. And when he reentered the living room, she felt as if she'd stepped back in time.

His hair was loose, shining, as it hung down his back. And a single wide black stripe of some kind of face paint slashed horizontally across his left cheekbone. The effect was simple, but so unexpected that she found it startling. She knew she had nothing to fear but, still, she had trouble catching her breath. He looked the very image of a proud warrior.

A sleeveless, waist-length tunic made of some kind of soft animal skin covered his chest, emphasizing his iron-like biceps. The breast area was fancily adorned with seashells that had been buffed to a sheen. His leggings were made of the same supple hide, fringed along the outside length of his leg. The moccasins he wore were beautifully beaded and it was obvious that hours had been put into the meticulous handwork.

The air in the room seemed to have completely disappeared. She didn't know what to say. The sight of him was awe-inspiring. And since *take me here, take me now,* would not be an appropriate comment, she decided to remain silent. But she was sure he must hear the hammering of her heart.

"These are for you," he offered her the box he had in his hand. "If you'd like to wear them, that is."

"What's in it?" she asked as she took the carved cedar box from him.

The latch was brass as were the hinges, and when she opened the lid, she gasped.

"They were Onna's," he told her.

Libby remembered the Mokee-kittuun word for mother.

"Her len-hok'sin. Moccasins. She wore them on special occasions. I thought you might like to borrow them."

"I'd love to." Her tone was hushed as she removed the moccasins from the box. The beading was delicate and colorful. "You're sure it's okay that I wear them?"

He nodded. "It's very much okay. Onna would be

honored to help you feel more a part of the celebration, I'm sure.''

Toeing off her shoes, Libby slipped her foot into one moccasin, the deerskin still whisper-soft against her skin. She tied it securely, then donned the other. She couldn't believe how comfortable the moccasins were. Or how beautiful. She felt honored that Rafe would trust her with what must be a cherished token from his past.

"Let's go," he said, reaching out his hand to her, "before we miss all the fun. And we shouldn't forget your jacket. The bonfire will be warm, but the walk there and back might get chilly."

Smiling, she slid her palm into his.

Even before they had actually reached the gathering, the beating of the drums and the rhythmic chanting reached down deep, seeming to touch Libby's very soul. The huge burning logs sent flames shooting high into the night sky. The group was larger than Libby expected, as what seemed to be over two hundred people milled around.

If it hadn't been for the fact that some of the participants wore regular clothing, she'd have truly believed she had been transported back into history. Many of the tribal members, like Rafe, were dressed in traditional garb. She saw men and women sporting furry animal skin capes and tanned-hide tunics, leggings and dresses.

The clothing was decorated with shells, glass beads and feathers. Some of their heads were bare, but others were dressed in adornments that ranged from a simple strip of beaver skin that had been painted and tied around the forehead to elaborate layers of feathers that flowed nearly to the ground. One dancer flaunted eight-inch-long porcupine quills that stuck straight from his head in a long, narrow row. Libby had no idea how the quills stood on end like they did, or how the man got the headdress to stay on his head.

"Amazing," she whispered to Rafe. "It's wonderful. Thanks for bringing me."

"I'm glad you wanted to come."

The awkwardness that had stretched taut between them eased then, vanished like a misty fog burned off by the first rays of the morning sun. Libby smiled and sighed deeply. It felt good to loosen what had been a tight grip on her anger.

"There's my sister."

Libby looked at the woman coming toward them. She thought she was as awed as she could possibly be after hearing the music and chanting, seeing the glorious costumes, but the woman in front of her was a sight to behold.

Her smooth, high cheekbones and large, expressive eyes, as dark as ebony, revealed beyond a shadow of a doubt that Native American blood flowed through her veins. Her hair was jet-black and hung to her waist. She was tall, long-legged and graceful. But what had Libby hard pressed to keep her jaw from hanging open was the woman's outfit.

The doeskin dress and matching cape were pure white, as were the beads and shells adorning the chest area and hem. Even the feathers hanging from the shoulders of the cape were opaline. Her moccasins were white as well, but unadorned. Her outfit was a stark contrast to her dark beauty.

"Libby," Rafe said, "I'd like you to meet my baby sister, Cheyenne Colton. Cheyenne, this is Libby Corbett."

Cheyenne's smile was serene, and when Libby reached

out to take the woman's hand, a wave of tranquillity washed over her.

"It's wonderful to meet you."

"I feel the same," Cheyenne said. "And, please, let me be the first to say that your father means a lot to the people of our tribe. He's done a great deal for us. I'm sure, in the end, truth will prevail and he'll be exonerated of all charges."

Libby could tell the speech was heartfelt. Tears burned her eyes, but she successfully thanked Rafe's sister without letting her emotions run rampant.

Cheyenne turned her gaze to Rafe. "Have you seen our brother?"

"Not yet."

She scanned the crowd. "He was with my husband the last time I saw them. They said they were hungry and were going to check out the food table."

Rafe chuckled. "That's typical, for both River and Jackson."

"All right now." Cheyenne's tone was infused with a good dose of both warning and teasing. "You can say what you want about River, but Jackson is the love of my life, remember."

Laughter rumbled deep in Rafe's chest and Libby felt her blood grow warm with the sound of it.

"Funny thing is," Rafe commented lightly, "the marriage sure didn't start out that way."

Intrigued by his statement, Libby simply stared, hoping someone would explain. Cheyenne's wide mouth drew back at one corner in wry response.

"Libby, my brother is teasing me because I got myself tangled up in a marriage of convenience. See, I married Jackson during that terrible Colton scandal last year. He was accused to trying to murder his uncle, but anyone who knows Jackson realizes that he'd never harm a hair on Joe's head. Or anyone else's, for that matter. The District Attorney was going to have me testify against Jackson…so I did the only thing an honorable girl could do. I married him.''

Rafe grinned at Libby. ''Jackson told Cheyenne he feared that her heathen brothers would use him as target practice.''

''He said no such thing,'' Cheyenne admonished. ''Jackson would never call you a heathen. Now, if you were to push me too far, *I* just might.''

Brother and sister shared an instant of humor, but then Libby witnessed as that moment metamorphosed into something else. Something touching. Poignant.

Cheyenne went to her brother and placed her palm against his chest. ''Although we both know you could never fit that description.''

She leaned closer then and kissed his cheek.

Rafe's jaw was tight, and intense emotion clouded his mahogany gaze. He swallowed, and did his best to smile at Cheyenne.

''I think I'll take a walk to look for River and Jackson,'' he said.

The two women stood near the outer rim of the gathering, a very good position to see all that was going on. One man, his face craggy with deep lines, seemed to hold entranced a group of children.

Finally Libby's curiosity got the better of her. ''Who is that?''

''Alex Featherstone,'' Cheyenne told her. ''He's a shaman. He offers the people medical advice. He's adept at herbal medicine. People go to him for counsel, for prayer. He's available to heal the mind, body and spirit. He's also a gifted storyteller, what you might call our oral historian. He's been educating our young people for more years than I can remember. Rafe and I both sat at that man's knee when we were kids. Alex makes sure everyone in the tribe knows where they come from and that we can be proud of the journey that's gotten us where we are.''

Libby loved the idea of oral history. In her world, it was a lost art.

"I've been visiting Alex lately," Cheyenne quietly admitted. She smiled. "There's quite a difference in listening to his stories and actually trying to learn them so I can recount them." She chuckled. "No matter how much time I spend with him, I'll never be able to weave tales like he does."

The women settled into a companionable silence as Libby watched a group of female dancers. The side-to-side steps they performed were simple, but the style used by each individual varied greatly from the next. Libby found her shoulders bouncing to the beat.

Soon she caught sight of Rafe talking to two men. River and Jackson, she surmised. Cheyenne saw her watching them.

"You've probably spent enough time with Rafe to discover that he's a complicated man."

Libby cut her eyes at the beautiful young woman, wondering about the meaning behind the out-of-the-blue remark. However, Cheyenne didn't take her eyes off her brothers and her husband.

"You have to understand," Cheyenne continued, "he's been through a lot, my oldest brother has. There are many torments…bad memories…in his heart and in his mind that he hasn't been able to release." Her tone softened as she added, "I hope that one day he'll find the strength to let go. Only then will he find peace and happiness.''

A dozen questions crowded in Libby's brain, but she didn't feel she had the right to ask even one of them. She had realized that Rafe was a complex man. She'd thought that very thing herself. And knowing the ordeals he'd faced just might help her to understand him.

However, she couldn't help but think that Rafe didn't care to be understood. Not by her, at least. He'd made that abundantly clear.

She wanted to confess all these thoughts to Cheyenne, but before she was able to formulate the right words, the crowd began to shift. The beat of the drums changed, the tempo quickened, and many of the men in the group made a wide circle around the bonfire. Rafe and River joined them.

''Oh, my,'' Cheyenne told Libby, her dark eyes glistening with sudden excitement. ''I think you'll enjoy this. If you'll excuse me.'' She left Libby standing there and went to watch the dance with her husband.

It was then that Rafe caught Libby's eye, his smile was broad, his body tall and proud, his smooth skin glowing in the firelight. Her pulse accelerated to match the steady beat of the drums.

She returned his smile, her eyes going wide with wonder as she realized she was about to observe a sight she would never forget. Energy, alive, almost tangible, trilled across every inch of her skin.

The men hooked their arms around the waists of those flanking them. In a single, unbroken circle, the dance began.

Twelve

In the luminous light of the bonfire, his skin took on the color of burnt sienna. The memory of sliding her fingertips over his satiny flesh hit her with great force. Her body flushed and her breath snagged as if her throat were lined with thorns.

She should put that night out of her head as if it had never happened, she knew. But doing so wasn't simple. In fact, it proved impossible. Unwittingly, the smile on her face waned as the present mingled with the past.

Desire curled low in her belly like a heated, fast-growing vine. The drum beat reminded her of the pounding of their hearts as they had made love. The fire was as deliciously hot as Rafe's touch had been. And the hazy smoke was just as enveloping as her yearning had been that night, washing over her, penetrating every nuance of her soul.

The circle of dancers rotated in a giant circle, and she

lost sight of Rafe for several moments. But then he rounded the fire, her gaze latching on to him as if she were starved for him. Although the thought disturbed her, that was exactly how she felt.

Starved for him.

How could her body and mind betray her so? She wanted to be strong. To keep herself safe. But the love she felt for him overpowered her need for emotional protection.

As broad and tall as he was, Rafe moved with grace. Lissome. Agile. Those words described him, too, Libby thought. She desperately tried to convince herself that it was the fire that caused this light-headed, overheated feeling…but it was too late to delude herself now. Rafe's dancing stirred her blood. Stirred her memories. Stirred her passion.

She nearly groaned with the wanting that possessed her so suddenly. A wanting that, in the midst of this chanting and percussion rhythm, seemed raw and primal.

The dance and the music ended abruptly, and the cheer that rose from the group of men was so unexpected that Libby started. Rafe jogged to her side, his very aura energized by the dance. She felt fairly scorched to the marrow of her bones.

"That was wonderful," she said, smiling, yet trying valiantly to hide the need thrumming through her being.

He only smiled, almost as if he didn't trust himself to speak. His passions, too, had been stimulated by the heady dance. Then she noticed the expression in his eyes. He was wrestling with his feelings just as hard as she was with her own.

Confusion muddled her thoughts. It was obvious that he wanted her. So why had he so harshly told her their night together had been a mistake?

Before she'd had time to ponder the question thoroughly, a touch on her forearm drew her gaze. Cheyenne's eyes glittered with what Libby could only describe as anticipation.

"Come," the young woman invited. "This is The Woman's Dance."

Libby's whole body resisted. "Oh, no...I couldn't."

Cheyenne grinned, coaxingly assuring her, "Sure, you can. The steps are simple. You'll catch on quickly."

"B-but..."

The protest died on her lips and she allowed herself to be led to the circle of women. Excitement skittered in the air, and Libby suddenly felt giddy with the idea of actually participating in the events of the evening.

Thankfully, the drum beats were slow, the accompanying flute, sweet, sonorous, and she watched Rafe's sister closely, mimicking each step, each move the woman made.

"Spring is the time for new beginnings," Cheyenne told her. "Renewal. Regeneration. A time when a woman needs to be—" her smile was slow and wry, her brows waggling suggestively "—enticing to the opposite sex. The Woman's Dance."

Her eyes wide as she realized the significance of the dance, Libby forced herself to concentrate on learning the foot placement.

"That's all there is to it. Simple, yes?" However, then Cheyenne's tone lowered wickedly. "But how you embellish the simple steps is up to you." Then her hips began to swing to the beat, her shoulders, too, as her gaze searched for and found her husband.

The movements of some of the women were quite suggestive. Risqué even.

Self-consciousness descended upon Libby. Like a

graceless, waddling duck among a flock of beautiful swans, she had never felt more out of place. It wasn't that she didn't have rhythm, or that she was completely clumsy. It was just that this was so new to her. And she was extraordinarily conscious of the message she might be conveying to Rafe. However, she wasn't a quitter. And she sure wasn't going to let a silly dance get the better of her.

Closing her eyes, she concentrated on the steps and let herself get lost in the primitive beat. She relaxed, and soon she felt comfortable enough to arch her spine, loosen her shoulders. She turned, dipped, let her bottom sway, to and fro to the sensuous beat.

She couldn't deny it. She felt sexy. Shamelessly so. The music filled her, strengthening her confidence and her assertiveness.

Tucking her chin close to her chest, she let her gaze saunter to Rafe, and her pulse accelerated when she saw that he seemed utterly captivated, his eyes locked on her.

He made her feel like the sole dancer, rather than one of many...as if she performed for him, alone. A shiver shimmied its way down the full length of her, head to foot.

She remembered the taste of his kiss, the secret scent of his skin, the heat of his touch, the sound of his heart thundering in his chest. She remembered it all. And she wished they were back at his house. In his room. Between his sheets. Kissing. Touching. Exploring. Making love.

Again, she was bewildered by why he'd proclaimed their night of passion to have been a mistake.

He had wanted her the night they had been intimate. And she knew beyond the shadow of a doubt that he wanted her now. So why had he denied her in the light of day?

She'd reacted to his rejection in anger, and she should hold tight to those hurt feelings. That was the surest way to protect herself.

She shouldn't care why he'd said what he'd said. She shouldn't wonder.

But she did.

My brother is a complicated man, Cheyenne had told Libby not too many minutes ago.

Rafe *was* complicated. Hadn't she come to that conclusion all on her own?

He was also too intriguing for words.

The music ended and the women dispersed, melting into the crowd. Libby felt awkward facing Rafe after the spectacle she'd just made of herself.

What should she say? Worse yet, what would he say?

Electricity seemed to throb in the heavy air. And he seemed just as unsure as she.

"Thirsty?"

She nodded.

They went to the refreshment table, and he picked up two cups of warm cider. The spicy apple and cinnamon flavor was delicious on her tongue.

"The Woman's Dance."

She heard the teasing in the low words he uttered.

"Why is it such hard work?"

From the lighthearted gleam in his dark and sexy gaze, she knew he didn't really mean the literal dance at all, but the man-woman dance performed by adults the world over. She didn't quite know how to answer him, so she simply remained quiet.

Unexpectedly, he took the cider from her and placed both cups on the table. He took her hand and led her away from the bonfire, where more music had begun to play. They walked up into the rocky foothills a short distance, the cool, satiny night wrapping around them.

"Careful," he said. "Don't trip."

She didn't intend to fall. On the rocks. Or for him.

Oh, who are you kidding? an insistent voice in her brain called to her. You've already fallen for the man. Hard enough to cause a concussion.

"Cold?"

"No." It was the first time she spoke since she'd executed that sexy little show for him. Her voice sounded all gravelly. Her nerves jangled. An invisible current hummed in the air. Something was about to happen. Why else would he be leading her into the darkness, away from the crowd?

When they neared a tall evergreen, he took her hand in his. He turned her to face him, the solid column of the tree supporting her back.

"I shouldn't want you," he said at last, leaning into her, refusing to meet her gaze.

The solid mass of him felt wonderful. So close. He traced light fingers along her jaw, down the length of her neck. She should be shouting at him, telling him to take his hands off her. But she didn't.

The clean cedar and leather smell of him mingled with the pungent evergreen boughs overhead, the scent of spicy apple cider. The night wind ruffled through his hair.

"I've tried not to want you."

His tone was thick. He bent toward her, the tip of his nose brushing high on her cheekbone. He inhaled then, slowly, languorously, breathing in her aroma, and Libby thought she'd never in her life experienced anything more erotic, more stirring.

"But, damn it, I just can't stop myself."

She should be angry. She should shove him away from her. Smack his face soundly.

He was admitting to wanting her and *not* wanting her. She should be repelled by the notion. Hadn't she been hurt by a man who had used her and abused her with the very same concept?

But something told her this was different. This battle Rafe was engaged in had little to do with her. He was fighting something inside himself. Some hidden enemy deep inside him bent on convincing him he shouldn't experience love or happiness…that he didn't deserve warmth and affection.

My brother is a complicated man…

At that moment, Libby realized that Cheyenne's words hadn't been an idle comment. They had been a warning of sorts. Gentle advice.

Right now, though, figuring out the complexities of him wasn't the priority in her mind. Tasting his kiss was.

His tunic was soft and supple in her fingers as she gathered it up and gave a pleading tug. His mouth slanted down over hers, and she slid her fingers over his scalp, combed them through his long hair, twisting the soft tresses over her palms, gently encouraging him to come closer and closer. The weight of him felt luscious, crushing her breasts, heating her with his nearness, churning her blood.

The warm tang of apple was on his lips, on his tongue. The delectable smell of him filled her lungs, inciting her lust for him.

She broke off the kiss long enough to utter a frantic whisper against his partly opened mouth. "Let's go back to your house."

Back to your bed.

The wantonness thickening her tone should have made

her ashamed. Where was her self-respect? Rafe had already said a relationship between them was impossible, yet here she was offering him her body. Again.

Pride be damned. She didn't care. She wanted this. She wanted him.

But his gaze cleared and his spine straightened. It was as if her suggestion had awakened him from his carnal stupor. He inched away from her.

"We can't do this. I can't, Libby. I can't do this to you. It's wrong."

Why? she wanted to scream. Why is it wrong?

His eyes refused to meet hers. And Libby should have felt hurt. But she didn't. She only felt sad. Yet, at the same time, she felt an overwhelming urge to reach out to him. However, she simply didn't feel he was ready to face whatever it was that tormented him.

"We have to go back," he told her. "Now. Before I change my mind."

One thing was certain. She'd realized that Rafe's rejecting her had little to do with her. He was battling demons. And whatever those demons were, they were keeping him from following his heart.

She followed him back toward the glow of the fire, back toward the buzz of the crowd, back toward the beating of the ancient native song. Libby feared that this failed intimacy between them would conjure that terrible awkwardness again, that the celebration would lose its magic. But as soon as they reached the gathering, she felt her excitement stir.

Cheyenne had taken a seat next to the old shaman, and the sounding of the drums faded as she began to speak.

"As many of you know," Rafe's sister began, men, women and children making themselves comfortable on the ground around her, "I have been visiting with Alex

Featherstone. He's been teaching me so much. I have been attempting to learn his stories." She smiled then. "It will take me many years, I'm sure. But one story—an important one—I have practiced especially for tonight. We have heard this story before many times." The young woman's gaze searched for and found Jackson's. "We must tell it to the people who are most important to us." She scanned the crowd, her hand splaying on her chest. "We must hold it in our hearts. We must remember."

The crowd grew hushed, expectant.

"Listen!" Cheyenne's tone swelled with insistence, her arms raising, palms facing one another, almost as if she were settling into a dramatic role. "Listen to my story!"

All murmurings died completely and all that could be heard was the snap and crackle of fire consuming wood. The very air took on an almost reverent feel, and goose-flesh coursed across every inch of Libby's skin.

"There was a time," the young woman said, her hands lowering to rest in her lap, "when Mother Earth was lush and rich and green. And The People flourished under her gentle care. Sister Sea provided plenty. Brother Forest yielded game and crops. Father Mountain spurted an abundance of pure, cool water. And all of these things The People enjoyed."

Libby cut her eyes at Rafe's profile. The fire high-lighted his high, proud cheekbones, his strong jaw. His mahogany eyes were leveled on his sister, his attention held rapt by her story.

"But then strangers arrived," Cheyenne said. "They came from the south. They came from the east. They came from the north. And they wanted all that Mother Earth had to give. They brought illness. And many of us sickened and died. But in spite of this, our great chief reached out his hand and offered to share all that we had. But he was struck down, his blood seeping into the dirt.''

The gazes of the children were wide.

"So The People took up arms and fought." Cheyenne paused. "But the outsiders were a formidable enemy. They used weapons we had never seen. Weapons that ripped the flesh even before the attacker could be observed. Many of our young warriors died. Too many to be counted.

"The outsiders offered us a piece of land. A small parcel in the rolling foothills from which we would not be allowed to roam. How could anyone own Mother Earth? Give her away in bits and pieces?''

Cheyenne's face expressed an incomprehension that made hot tears spring to Libby's eyes.

"How could the foreigners offer what was not theirs to give?'' Dramatically, the young woman reached up and touched her chin in deep contemplation. "They could not, The People decided. So the warring continued. But then The Big Battle sent nearly all of our braves to The Other Side. The river turned crimson with their blood. Our people were a hair's breadth from complete annihilation. That is not what The Great Spirit wanted for The People.''

She straightened, then, her shoulders leveling with what could only be described as sensibility. Not defeat. Never defeat.

"The wise Elders gathered together,'' she continued. "They decided to accept the offer of land—the offer of peace—that the outsiders had presented. They also decided that, in order to survive, they would open their arms in invitation to the surviving members of other tribes. Our small parcel of land would become a safe haven. And The People came. Women and fatherless children, grandfathers and grandmothers, wounded braves, all came from near and far. We were no longer members of neighboring tribes. We were one family. Born of the blood shed by our warriors. We became Mokee-kittuun. People of the Red River.''

Tears ran freely down Libby's cheeks now. And she realized she wasn't the only one in the crowd who wept.

''But this is not a sad tale,'' Cheyenne said, her mouth widening into a bright and glorious smile. ''This is a story of hope. We are a people who thrive. We are a people who prosper. And grow. We have sent doctors and lawyers and business owners out into the world. The Mokee-kittuun are teachers and artists, engineers and scientists. We have survived. We can be proud of who we are. Where we are. We can be proud of our past, and look confidently, optimistically into our future.''

Cheyenne paused for only a moment. Finally she had reached the end of her story. ''We remember our past in order to honor our ancestors.'' Her gaze fanned across the faces of the tribal members, settling on her brother's. ''But we should not let the past hinder our future.''

Libby sensed there was a gentle message being conveyed. A personal message from sister to brother, although Rafe showed no sign of it.

Then Cheyenne let her dark eyes slide to the faces of the children in the very front of the crowd. She smiled. ''We must remember,'' she told them.

For several moments no one seemed to move a muscle. The whole tribe seemed to be basking in the pride of their past. Libby didn't blame them. Had it been her past, she'd have basked as well.

Her gaze lifted to Rafe's face. A smile shadowed the corners of his mouth.

''My sister's going to do all right,'' he said. ''She was

a little nervous about studying with Alex Featherstone. Becoming a shaman will take a lot of her time. It's been a big decision for her to make.''

"I can imagine." Libby shook her head in amazement. "She told me she was learning the man's stories. But I didn't know she was studying to become a shaman."

Rafe's gaze arced affectionately to Cheyenne who was talking quietly to the group of children gathered round her knees.

"When she approached the Elders a couple of months ago with her decision," he told her, "they showed their faith in her by presenting her with the dress and cloak she's wearing." He then added, "It was a gift they had been waiting to offer her. They believe in her."

People began to say their goodbyes. The celebration was ending.

On the way back to Rafe's house, Libby realized how special the evening had been. It would be a night she'd remember forever. She felt so blessed to have been included in this spring ceremony of thanksgiving and remembrance. Having the chance to see Rafe dance had been a special gift. And participating in The Woman's Dance had been a wonderful experience. The expression of concentrated yearning in Rafe's dark gaze as he'd watched her would be forever emblazoned in her mind.

Yes, this was a night she would hold deep in her heart.

As she pondered, however, she couldn't help but feel curious about some things. Why would Cheyenne feel compelled to offer her advice about Rafe's complex nature? And what had happened to him in the past that continued to affect him now? What was it that he was unable to let go of? And why?

And why—when he'd kissed her tonight by the evergreen tree, when he'd so obviously wanted her—had he said that intimacy between them was wrong? That he couldn't ''do this'' to her?

Libby sensed that all these bits of information were like pieces to a puzzle. But for the life of her, she was unable to make them all fit.

Thirteen

As soon as the sun had come up over the horizon, Rafe
had asked Libby to accompany him on a trek up into the
foothills. She'd willingly agreed, but when she'd inquired
about their destination, he'd purposefully kept his answer
vague.

The jackets they wore protected them from the foggy
chill that had rolled in off the Pacific in the wee hours
of the morning. In an hour or so, the sun would most
likely burn off the haze and warm the air. Maybe twice
in all the years he'd lived in Prosperino and Crooked
Arrow had he seen snow fall this close to the ocean, but
in the damp month of March, fog was common.

Rafe was wholly uncertain about what he intended to
do this morning. Taking Libby to this special place could
very well be a mistake. And after the way she'd reacted
to the tribal celebration last night—he could close his
eyes and see the excitement lighting her beautiful face—

he didn't want her to be disappointed if they reached the mouth of the cave and some inner voice told him to go no further. She was not Mokee-kittuun, and the cave was of great importance to his people. Rafe would have to pay particular attention to his intuition.

Instinct. Perception. Inner voice. These were all important aspects of being human. Being connected to The Great Father. Being connected to the universe. Most people didn't take the time to simply listen to that tiny spark of godliness they were born with. And in Rafe's estimation, those people were foolish.

"I had a wonderful time last night," Libby said, her tone muffled by the heavy moisture hanging in the air.

"I'm glad. So did I."

The celebration had taken on new meaning for him as he'd watched the anticipation and wonder fairly glimmer in her aqua eyes. When he'd danced around the flames, his steps had been more sure, more precise, than ever before, and he knew in his heart that had been because Libby's gaze had been on him. And seeing her join the other women, seeing her body sway and roll to the sensuous beat...

He'd broken out in a cold sweat, his need had been so great. Going against everything he knew was right, he'd taken her hand and slipped into the dark cover of the night, away from the crowd, the yearning in him had been that insistent.

And after they had returned to his home, the very air had vibrated with sexual current. She'd have come to him. To his bed. All he'd have had to do was give her a look, a touch. However, he'd controlled himself. He'd had no idea how, but he was proud that he had.

Knowing that a relationship between them was impossible, he believed with all his heart that physical intimacies should be avoided. The battle now was in forcing the needs of his body to surrender to his beliefs.

"The tribe is—"

A gasp issued from her as she lunged forward. He reached out to her, grabbing her arm, and when momentum continued to carry the left half of her body, he reacted with swift movement. The incident was over in the blink of an eye. But the two of them were left standing close.

He noted the surprise in her eyes, how her scrumptious lips formed a small circle. The moment hovered, energy pulsing. However, what captured every nuance of his attention was the warm roundness of her breasts as they pressed against his forearm.

"I should learn to pick up my feet," she said, inching from him, consciously tugging at the hem of her jacket. "I'm all right. Thanks."

He didn't want to release her, she felt so damned good up next to him. But there was nothing else for him to do except back off.

Rafe took her hand. "These rocks can be dangerous." Steadying her was a practical thing to do, he decided. But a quiet voice told him he only wanted to feel her skin next to his own.

"As I was going to say before I nearly fell and broke my silly neck," Libby continued, seemingly at ease to be holding hands with him, "is that the tribe seems to be very close-knit."

He nodded. "We're more than merely members of the same tribe. More than just neighbors. We're as devoted to each other's welfare as blood kin would be."

Interest lit her expression.

"We think of ourselves as family," he told her. "So much so, that there was a time in our history when taking a wife or husband from within the clan was forbidden. It was looked upon almost like incest.''

"But how did people find their partners?''

Rafe smiled. ''At ceremonies just like the one you attended last night. Celebrating is an important part of our culture. People would come from all over to share the fun. Meet new people. Find a mate.'' He shrugged. ''The custom of strictly marrying outside of the tribe has died out now. I'm sure that had something to do with all those foreigners showing up.''

He grinned, hoping she would catch on that he was teasing. She did.

They walked several steps in silence. Then she said, ''I like the idea of having lots of family around. Not having any brothers or sisters made growing up pretty lonely at times.''

A painful memory knifed from the back of Rafe's brain. He remembered those lonely hours spent worrying about his younger brother after Curtis James had wrenched River out of Rafe's life.

He shoved the thought from him. He knew conjuring up his bad memories hadn't been Libby's intent.

''Well,'' he said slowly, ''I've learned over the years that friends really can become like family. I've known Blake Fallon for years and years. He's like a brother to me.''

Birds of a feather. That was what Rafe and Blake had been. As teens, the two of them had been full of anger and raging to rebel. Against everything and everyone. And for a time, they had done just that.

''Unfortunately, I never have been one to make friends very easily.''

The sorrow in her tone made Rafe forget all about the pain of his own past.

"What do you mean?" The question pitched forth before he could even think to stop it. She was beautiful. Intelligent. Fun-loving. Inquisitive. All those things that popular people were. He couldn't imagine her not having a boatload of friends, but he did recall her saying once that she'd had a lonely childhood.

The shadow that crept over her face made him frown.

"I didn't have what you'd call a normal childhood," she began. "You see, I suffered with a severe speech impediment. It was so bad, in fact, that I refused to talk at all except to Mom and Dad. I felt ashamed, from my earliest memories. I didn't want to go out. Didn't want to communicate." The mass of her hair bobbed when she shook her head. "I *couldn't* communicate. That was the thing."

She sighed. "My parents loved me. And they did everything in their power to protect me. My mother was everything to me. My parent, my friend, my teacher, my playmate. We'd play dress-up, and she'd get right down on the floor with me and play with my dolls. We created skits, and she taught me to bake. Of course, Dad had to work to pay the bills. But he joined in with our fun each evening. We'd dance." Her mouth curled at one corner. "I remember standing on his feet as we waltzed around the living room."

She took a moment to pinch her bottom lip between her teeth. "Oh, but they worried about me. I know they did. They contacted specialists, took me to therapists, doctors. Always looking for some way to fix my problem." The edgy chuckle she expelled contained not an ounce of humor. "The last woman we went to see grew so frustrated that she blamed me for not trying hard enough. My self-esteem took such a beating that Mom and Dad finally just closed ranks around me."

Rafe stopped walking. "We don't have far to go," he told her, reluctantly letting go of her hand. "But let's sit here and rest a minute."

With no argument, Libby perched herself on the rocky outcropping.

"What do you mean that they 'closed ranks'?" he asked.

Love shined bright in her eyes. "Mom and Dad became my protective wall against life. They loved me and nurtured me. They let me know I was the light of their lives, and it didn't matter that I couldn't speak clearly."

Obviously, her childhood experience and the speech impediment with which she'd suffered had taken a huge toll on her. Rafe could see it in her rounded shoulders, in the ache expressed on her face, in the clouds in her eyes. Like her parents had done, he wanted to close ranks. To gather her up in his arms and protect her.

"Your speech," he began, "is…" He lifted a palm as he searched for the correct word. "Clear. Eloquent." His head shook. "How…?"

Libby looked around them. "The fog is gone. And I'm rested. Should we move on?"

"Sure." Automatically, he got up and started over the rocky ground. "But don't think you're going to leave me wondering."

She chuckled, and Rafe believed there wasn't prettier music to be heard.

"I wouldn't dream of it." She trudged up one particularly jagged section of ground, accepting the helping hand he offered her. "My father brought home a man one day. I was eleven at the time. My parents told me right up front that Dr. Ericson was a specialist. At first, I was angry with them. I felt betrayed. I didn't want to face more humiliation. But Dr. Ericson quickly told me that I didn't have to say a single word to him if I didn't want to.''

Rafe didn't understand. "But how did he intend to help you?''

Again, she laughed. "He taught me the anatomy of speech. He taught me how the muscles in my mouth and throat work to make sound. He seemed more like a science teacher to me than a therapist. And he was funny. He made me laugh. When I was finally comfortable around him, I began to practice. He worked diligently with me for eight years.''

Her hand felt good in his. And the pride that came with her success made her beam.

"I still run into problems," she told him. "In times of overwhelming stress. But I just calm myself and perform the exercises that Dr. Ericson taught me.''

Then Rafe remembered the night she'd been attacked at the burger joint. She had stumbled verbally during and after the incident.

"All in all," Libby said, "I didn't have it so bad. So many of the doctors gave up on me. So I endured a little teasing from the neighborhood children…''

He knew she was making light of what she'd been forced to tolerate. But hearing about her experience did help him to understand the doubts she had in herself.

Rafe felt her eyes on him as she asked, "But don't you think we all face bad experiences as kids? I'm sure you understand what I mean.''

She was probing. Trying to get him to talk about himself, about his childhood.

Bringing her here had been a way for him to share with her when, in his mind, there was so little of himself that he felt able to reveal. This cave—this sacred place—

and the information harbored deep under the earth, was something he was pleased to be able to offer her.

His horrible memories had to remain locked inside, but he could give her a better understanding of his theory about the case they were working on. And hopefully she'd realize that, by bringing her here, he was proving his trust in her.

"I do understand." And he left it at that. "This is what I wanted you to see." He pointed to the slit in the rock that was the mouth of the cave.

Although there was a smile on her face, her eyes conveyed her disappointment that he'd once again sidestepped her attempts to get him to talk about himself.

"Come on." He squeezed through the opening, beckoning her to follow.

The morning light arrowed into the opening, lighting their way down the narrow corridor.

"What is this?" she asked. "Someplace you used to hang out?" Mirth skirted her tone when she added, "My dad built me a treehouse in our backyard, but this is way cooler than any wooden fort."

He shared her soft laughter, but refused to answer her questions. Instead, he urged her onward.

"Feels like we're descending," she observed.

"We are."

When the tunnel made an abrupt turn, Libby seemed to grow wary. "Shouldn't we have a flashlight?"

He grinned, assuring her, "We're fine. We're almost there."

The final fifty feet were traveled in a deep gray darkness at a decline that had them leaning into their heels.

"Rafe?"

"Almost there," he murmured, the feeling of reverence, the need for quiet tones coming upon him suddenly, just as it always did when he came here.

The passageway opened into a large chamber and he heard Libby's indrawn breath. It was an awesome sight. Rays of sunlight shafted down from openings high above, illuminating the cave's colorful walls, layers of rock in hues ranging from rusty red to mossy green and slate gray. The floor was smooth and nearly level.

"It's magical," Libby breathed on a exhaled sigh. "Look, I've got goose bumps."

The way she whispered revealed that she, too, sensed the holiness of the place.

"The light seems like liquid the way it cascades like that. Oh, my. It's beautiful."

Reaching across her chest, she rubbed her hands over her upper arms. Rafe watched her closely, wanting to see her first impressions of this most hallowed place. She was too busy looking all around her to notice him observing her.

"Listen. I hear water running." Delight shone in her gaze, on her face. She took a single step into the chamber and stopped. "This place is enchanted. There's magic in the air. Can't you feel it?"

Her eyes were round. On him now. And self-consciousness tickled the tiny hairs on the back of his neck.

This was a serene place, a divine sanctuary. He'd always thought that. So did the rest of his tribe. However, at this moment, it *did* seem enchanted. But Rafe silently surmised that it was Libby who had brought in the magical quality.

"What is this place?"

"The first time I was brought here, I was just about three years old," he told her. "For a naming ceremony.

I came with several other children about my age. A fire was roaring there.'' He pointed to a blackened spot in the middle of the cave. ''And Alex Featherstone chanted a blessing and gave all the children their names.''

A frown bit into her brow. ''You didn't have a name? But what did your parents, your family and friends, call you before that?''

''You don't understand. My name was Rafe, of course,'' he explained. ''But many tribes have a custom to give their children another name. An Indian name. And often it's a name that is associated with a totem. A symbol. And that symbol often takes the form of an animal. But since my family already had an animal totem associated with our name—''

''Running Deer,'' Libby supplied.

Rafe nodded.

''So what name did the shaman choose for you?'' Then she rushed to add, ''If you're allowed to tell me.''

He had to chuckle. ''It's mine to share with whomever I wish.'' Glancing over at the darkened circle on the floor, he remembered experiencing the pride he'd felt of being Mokee-kittuun.

Alex's chanting had filled him with awe and, yes, a little fear, too. When he'd been motioned forward, Rafe hadn't hesitated, knowing that his parents looked on. He'd forced his backbone straight. The fire had been hot, the smoke, acrid. Alex's firm hands on his shoulders had pivoted him to face the onlookers.

Rafe remembered the love shining in his mother's gaze and the pride lighting his father's piercing dark eyes.

His mouth and throat going dry, Rafe realized in that very instant that he *did* have a memory of his father. Ridge Running Deer had been pleased with his son the night Rafe had received his Mokee-kittuun name.

This insight caused his insides to quake. His knees went weak. His hands trembled.

Libby's hand on his arm plucked him out of the past. "Are you okay?"

Her question was whispered, as if even in her alarm she couldn't bring herself to speak in anything other than hushed tones.

Rafe cleared his throat. "Tipaakke Shaakhan is the name Alex gave me that night," he told her. "It means Dark Wind."

He'd often wondered if the shaman had some ethereal knowledge of how life was going to turn out for Rafe. Many times while living under Curtis James's roof, and even after returning to the rez without his brother, Rafe had felt as if a dark and haunting wind blew through him.

Seeming to sense his mood, Libby commented, "A little depressing for a child of three, don't you think?" She smiled, her mouth cocking up wryly.

He let go of the past completely then, chuckling at her query.

She made her way deeper into the chamber. "So naming ceremonies are held here."

"As well as weddings and baptisms and—"

She whirled around, delighted. "Why, it's a church."

"It is a sacred place." He nodded.

"You know," she said, her manner easy, her tone light, "all this talk of naming ceremonies makes me wonder…"

Rafe stilled, pondering what she might be up to.

"You're very proud of your heritage," she continued. "Have you ever considered taking back your Mokee-kittuun name? You could be Rafe Running Deer again, you know. I'd be happy to file the proper paperwork for you."

Was she probing again, trying to get him to reveal his past? The guilelessness in her expression told him, no. She was simply offering a suggestion that had suddenly popped into her head. And what an amazing suggestion it was, too. But before he could consider it fully, she cocked her head.

"I do hear water, don't I?"

"You do." He took her hand, and doing so felt like the most natural thing in the world. "Come on. I have something to show you."

Her gaze glittered with anticipation. "There's more to see?"

Oh, but she was lovely. He said nothing, only tugged on her hand.

Rafe led her through the long cave. At the far end the sound of surging water was louder. The tumbling stream couldn't actually be seen, but he took her to a small body of water, its glassy surface reflecting the rock formations of the ceiling.

"Oh." She reached down and scooped up a handful. "It's cold." The drops falling from her fingers sent out ever-widening concentric circles across the smooth surface.

"That's what I want you to see." With a lift of his chin, he indicated the wall on the far side of the pool.

"What am I supposed to be seeing?" she asked, studying the rock face.

"It's a fault. A cross section of it, actually."

She nodded mildly, not yet understanding the significance of what was in front of her.

"The fault runs directly through the cave," he continued. "See how one side is shoved up over the other?"

"I do." She turned to look at the opposite wall. "Yes, I do see it. What does it mean?"

"Well, that running water you hear is part of the aquifer that supplies the water for the area. I'm sure of it."

She shot him a look of bewilderment. "But that water is moving. I thought an aquifer was like a huge underground lake. Am I wrong?"

"The earth is a living, moving thing, Libby. It shifts and seizes, changes constantly. I think a tremor rolled through here hundreds, maybe thousands of years ago. I think the earth heaved and I think the aquifer was tipped."

From her expression, she seriously considered all he said.

Finally, she lifted an apologetic palm. "I don't understand what you're trying to tell me."

"The aquifer flows in a southerly direction. Away from Crooked Arrow."

Her head bobbed. "Toward Prosperino." Awareness dawned. "Toward Hopechest Ranch." She blinked. "This has to do with your idea that someone meant to contaminate the reservation. If someone dumped DMBE, not knowing that the aquifer flows to the south, they wouldn't know that the chemicals they dumped would flow away from Crooked Arrow and straight toward the children's ranch, then on to Prosperino."

Rafe just looked at her. He said, "I wanted you to see it. I wanted you to understand."

"I do. But, Rafe, you still haven't convinced me that someone wanted to pollute Crooked Arrow. What kind of proof do you have?"

Protecting those he loved was paramount to Rafe. He'd spent his childhood shielding his little brother. And when Curtis James dumped Rafe and Cheyenne at the rez, driving away with River, Rafe had then turned his protective instincts toward his baby sister. He'd spent a lot of years looking after Cheyenne.

But he trusted Libby. He trusted her a great deal. She could handle what he was about to tell her. Surely she could. Couldn't she?

With some hesitation, he said, "My sister told me."

"Cheyenne?" Agitation had Libby's words coming fast and furious. "But how does she know? Did she overhear something? Witness something? What?"

Rafe scrubbed his fingers over his chin, still unsure of how much to reveal.

Libby was an intelligent woman. She'd proved that. She was honorable, loyal to her father, a good person. And the interest she'd shown in his heritage demonstrated that she wasn't like those whites who look down on Native Americans. She'd earned his respect. And his trust. Still…

He wavered. He lifted his chin and looked her directly in the eye. "Cheyenne has a gift."

Libby went utterly still and silent.

"My sister possesses the blessing of sight. She sees things, has visions. The images aren't always clear. When she tapped into what was happening, she didn't see faces or names. But when she came to me she was sure that someone was trying to poison our land."

Libby went quiet. What was she thinking? Rafe wondered. What thoughts were running through her head? Would she believe him or proclaim him a gullible and ignorant heathen?

"And since I'm coming clean," he continued. "There's one more thing I need to tell you." He sighed, hoping that in the days and weeks they had spent together, she'd have come to know him well enough to have faith in what he was about to reveal. That she wouldn't doubt him because of who he was or where he came from.

He swallowed, moistened his lips. "Last year I was filling in at Springer as a security guard. They call me when they're shorthanded. Anyway, during my stint there, I overheard two execs talking. I heard one of them say that the strip of land on Crooked Arrow needed to be purchased at any and all costs. I didn't know at the time who the men were. But I saw the picture of one of the men in the paper recently."

She hadn't moved, hadn't even blinked.

"That man was Todd Lamb."

A tiny whoosh of air rushed between Libby's lips when she gasped. "You think *he's* behind all this?" Her gaze lowered to the floor. "What if it's bigger than just him, though? What if…what if those running the company…" Her tone was as crackly as dried paper. It was clear that she didn't want to believe any of what was quickly becoming plain fact. "This can't be. It just can't be. My father worked his whole life for that company. Gave them everything he had to give."

Lifting her beautiful, pained eyes to Rafe, she asked, "How could this happen?"

Fourteen

The hike back to Rafe's house seemed to take no time at all to Libby. But that was probably because her thoughts were in such chaos.

Cheyenne possessed the gift of sight, Rafe had said. Libby had seen gaudily clad women at flea markets set up in San Francisco doing all they could to lure passersby to have their fortunes told, to have their love lives laid bare, or have their tarot cards read. Too practical and grounded in reality to give such matters much thought, Libby had never paid them much attention.

However, having seen Rafe's sister at the celebration last night, having talked to the woman, having heard and been touched by the poignant history she'd recounted, Libby doubted that Cheyenne's psychic gift had much to do with those flea market fortune-tellers. From what Rafe had told her this morning in the cave, his sister had spent months coming to the decision of apprenticing under the

Mokee-kittuun shaman, Alex Featherstone. Libby seriously doubted that Alex or Cheyenne would ever really profit from their calling—and that's what she concluded it must be: a true spiritual calling.

Besides, Cheyenne's gift must have been well known among the tribe for quite some time. How else would the Elders have had that gorgeous ceremonial costume ready and waiting should she decide to become a shaman? And all those people had hung on Cheyenne's every word last night, confidence and trust and something else as well— *gratitude*—shining in their faces.

If the whole of the Mokee-kittuun tribe believed that Rafe's sister had been blessed with a special gift, who was Libby to doubt it?

Cheyenne had "seen" that someone was trying to poison the water and land of Crooked Arrow. And Rafe had showed her the heaved fault that he suspected tipped the aquifer and sent the current rushing toward Hopechest Ranch where all those poor children had been hospitalized and evacuated for weeks, toward the town of Prosperino where the water had been tested and found to have traces of the chemical as well. Yet no one on the reservation had become ill.

Rafe's theory made a great deal of sense.

The notion that Springer could be attempting to frame her father for a purposeful chemical contamination was simply flabbergasting to her. How could she fight an entire company? Self-doubt swirled in her like muddy waters and she did what she could to dam them.

Since learning about the computerized journal that her father denied generating, Libby had realized that *someone* was trying to set him up to take the fall. Someone was attempting to sabotage his good name and blame him for something he didn't do. Could that someone be Todd Lamb?

The fact that Rafe had overheard an important conversation, yet he hadn't told her, grated on her. His ranch house was in sight when Libby pinched at his jacket sleeve, pulling him up short.

"Why didn't you tell me?" she asked, irritation flaring. "Why didn't you say you thought Todd Lamb was out to get my father?"

The muscles of Rafe's face were taut, and she got the sense that he'd been steeling himself for this.

"I did tell you that someone was trying to contaminate our land, Libby."

"But you never said why you thought that. How could I take your suspicions seriously when you didn't provide an identity or a motive?"

The corded sinew at the back of his jaw relaxed. "What could I say? How would you have reacted had I told you my information came from an Indian psychic?"

He had her there. If he'd spilled that story the first day they had met, she'd probably have shown him to the door with a polite, "Thanks, but no thanks."

"But you overheard Todd Lamb say he wanted that land at all costs. That's concrete proof that he's a suspect. That's hard evidence—"

"That's hearsay."

She frowned, reaching up to press her hand to her chest. "It hurts me to think you didn't trust me with what you knew."

"It wasn't that at all, Libby. You have to believe me."

"Then what was it? Help me to understand. My father is in deep trouble here, and now I find out you've been withholding information for weeks."

"Libby..." He exhaled, redirecting his gaze to some far-off place on the horizon.

She loved hearing him say her name. Loved the way it seemed to float off his lips. He caressed her name when he uttered it.

Finally his eyes returned to her face. "It's not that I didn't trust you. It's that I didn't know if you'd trust me. I didn't know if you'd believe what I had to say."

For an instant that idea threw her. "But..." Both of her shoulders lifted. "What had I done to lead you to think I wouldn't believe you?"

"You're not hearing me," he said dully. "It wasn't you." He sighed. "Look, Libby, when you live in this skin—" he raked the backs of his fingers down his jaw "—you learn that people are unconcerned with your opinions. That people disbelieve what you say. That people are uncaring of your needs and your wants and your hopes and your dreams. People just discount you. That's the way it is. The way it's always been."

He was talking about living with the prejudices of others. Living in a world where much of the population had preconceived notions about who you were and what you stood for based simply on the color of your skin or the shape of your features.

"It was me," he said. "I needed to learn that *you* would trust *me*."

She could argue her point further. She could easily sustain her hurt feelings. She could remind him that he knew David Corbett. That he knew her father had helped the Mokee-kittuun people procure jobs at Springer and advance in those jobs. Then she could point out that she was her father's daughter, and that the walnut rarely fell far from the tree.

But calling attention to all that would only make Rafe feel worse for not having confided in her sooner.

"Rafe, when we look at people we shouldn't see the color of their skin or the shape of their eyes or the texture of their hair. People are people. Some are good and some are bad. It doesn't matter their race. It has to do with the heart that beats inside them."

Cynicism edged his tone as he said, "That's easy for you to say. Your skin is white. You can go anywhere, talk to anyone, and you'll be respected."

What he said was true. Very true. And suddenly the need to apologize welled up in Libby.

"Let me tell you a little story," he said. "After my mother died and I returned to the reservation to live, I was filled with rage. And I was looking for some way to release it. Well, I found myself a friend. A good friend who was just as angry as I was. We took to joy-riding around Prosperino on motorcycles. Motorcycles that we stole. We were picked up by the police more than once. And each time, my friend was released to his guardian. Because his skin was white and his family had money and prestige, he was given preferential treatment. And me? I was held in that jail cell. Waiting for hours, and sometimes days, before I was allowed to see anyone from the rez."

Libby supposed that when Rafe had had this experience, the police department had most probably been filled with predominantly white officers. She strongly suspected it remained that way even today. But she hated to think that race bias had been their motivation in the treatment Rafe had received.

"Maybe they didn't keep you there because you're Indian," she said. "Maybe they were trying to teach you a lesson. Let you see where your behavior was taking you.''

But clearly Rafe didn't believe that, and the look on his face told her that she'd be a fool to even consider the notion.

''Oh, they taught me a lesson, all right. They taught me that they think I don't deserve the same treatment as others.''

All Libby wanted to do was reach out to Rafe, to somehow soothe the wounds that had been inflicted on him while growing up in a discriminatory society. However, one thing she'd learned about him was that he was a proud man. She feared he wouldn't accept any comfort she might offer.

Softly she said, ''You told me before that Blake Fallon was your best friend, like a brother to you. Is he the person you're talking about? The one who stole motorcycles and got into trouble with you?''

Rafe nodded. A cool Pacific breeze whipped at his hair, blowing it across his face. Reaching up, he swiped it back in one fluid movement.

''I don't blame Blake. He felt terrible every time he was released, every time that metal door closed between us, me on the inside, him on the outside. I don't blame Joe Colton, either. He was just doing what he could for Blake.''

''Joe Colton? *The* Joe Colton was Blake's guardian?''

At the mention of the man's name, Libby remembered the scandal. Over a year ago someone had tried to murder Joe Colton, the wealthiest resident of Prosperino. She also recalled that Blake's father, Emmett had been the guilty party.

Again, Rafe nodded. ''Blake lived with the Coltons for several years.''

Silence settled over them, and Libby thought the conversation had petered out. Rafe took a step toward home, but then he stopped and turned to face her yet again.

"I remember," he said, "when an officer told Joe Colton he'd be doing Blake a big favor if he kept him away from me. A knife slicing into my gut wouldn't have injured me worse."

"Oh, Rafe." She couldn't have stopped those words from coming had her life depended on it. Without thought, she reached out and took his hand in hers. If he rejected her comfort, she'd deal with it. But she simply had to express her compassion.

Their fingers laced together in a perfect fit.

"I'm sorry," she said. "I'm so sorry."

"I felt so damned ashamed of what I'd done, of the disgrace I'd placed on my name. Oh, not on the James name. I don't give a spit about that. But I'd always thought of myself as a Running Deer. And everyone knew I was a thief. You asked why I hadn't changed my name back to Running Deer. Well, that's why. Shame."

Libby thought her heart was going to wrench clean in two. Her very soul ached for Rafe. For what he'd gone through, for all he'd endured.

"You were just a kid," she pointed out. "And you said yourself, you were angry. You didn't have any other outlet. Your parents were gone. Rafe, you did the best you could."

"Running around thieving and getting into trouble was not the best I could do. And when that cop looked at me with such contempt and said that my best friend would be better off without me...well, all I can say is from that day on, I never took another thing that didn't belong to me. I've never broken another law." His tone was dry as he added, "I don't even drive over the speed limit."

Softly she said, "Your parents would be proud of the man you are."

He didn't respond. Libby didn't even know if he'd heard her. She also didn't know when he'd released her hand, but they started off toward the house. Thoughts churned in Libby's head.

She'd lived such a sheltered life compared to him. She'd spent her childhood and her teen years almost cloistered in a cocoon woven for her by her loving parents. Whereas, Rafe had lost his father at a very early age. His mother had been forced to leave the reservation to find work. She'd married an alcoholic, a mean drunk, Libby remembered. Rafe had faced adversity and strife. He'd faced the kind of hardship that fostered anger and resentment bone deep, and it had affected him. Enough to have caused him to rebel against it.

Once again, Libby wondered exactly what had happened to cause such anger in him.

There are many torments, Cheyenne's words wafted through Libby's mind, *bad memories…in his heart and in his mind…that he hasn't been able to release.*

The years Rafe had spent with Curtis James, Libby suspected, were the key to unlocking all those many torments. If she could somehow unlock them, maybe, just maybe, she could persuade him to release them. Maybe she could liberate him from all the dark and plaguing memories.

The computer expert sent by Libby's San Francisco law firm was waiting for them when Libby and Rafe arrived at the courthouse. Her name was Susanna Hash, and she looked about twelve years old. She was petite and slender. Her blond hair was cut in a short bob and she chewed the gum in her mouth with such enthusiasm that it snapped and cracked.

"Brought all the equipment I need," Susanna told Libby. "If you can find me a place to set up, and give me the addie for Springer's server, I'll be set."

"Addie?" Libby's eyebrows raised with her question.

"Internet address. Also known as an ISP." The girl's speech slowed, as if she thought Libby might be some kind of moron. "Internet Service Protocol."

"The server Springer uses is located in San Diego," Libby felt compelled to warn.

Susanna grinned. "No prob. Doesn't matter if the actual database is in China. All I need is the addie and I can get in." She shrugged. "'Course, I could get in without it, but it would take a while. And you do want this to be legit, right?"

Prob? Legit? Libby wondered what kind of expert she'd been sent.

Libby stressed, "Absolutely legitimate. In every sense of the word."

The girl snapped her gum as she grinned. "It will be, I promise. If someone from Springer so much as attempted to illegally mess with that database, I'll know about it. And so will you."

"Okay, then, let's go to the hotel and get you set up," Libby told the girl. "You can follow us there."

"Oh, before we go—" Susanna's pent-up energy had her lifting up onto her toes, rocking back onto her heels "—I have a message for you."

"A message?" Libby tossed a quick look at Rafe, then back at the young woman.

"The senior partner sends a greeting," Susanna told her. "Mr. Adams also says that if you need more help, he'll send someone. Whatever you need, just call."

A gray cloud descended on Libby. So the senior partner of her firm, like her own father, didn't believe she was capable of handling this case alone. Plastering a smile on her mouth, she told the girl, "Thanks. I'll keep that in mind."

On the way to the car, Rafe said, "I thought they were sending a skilled specialist. You sure this...um, young woman is experienced enough for what we need?"

Libby lifted one shoulder. "Apparently she's the best. Graduated from MIT top of her class. I was told if anyone could root out computer sabotage, she could do it."

"She seems like just a silly kid to me." Rafe started the engine.

Chuckling, Libby said, "Me, too. Let's hope we're both wrong."

Her naked skin tasted honey-sweet. Her silky hair, the mass of it fanned out on the ground above her head, glowed like shiny new pennies in the firelight. She arched her back, lifted her bare breasts as an offering, and he took one dusky nipple between his teeth. A moan gathered in the back of her throat, and he was certain he would lose all control.

Her tone was a rich and husky whisper. "Rafe."

With a gasp, he opened his eyes and sat up, breaking the bonds of sleep. Sweat chilled his skin. He threw back the covers, got out of bed and donned a pair of loose flannel pajama bottoms.

These dreams were going to be the death of him.

The sun hadn't yet risen above the horizon, so when he opened his bedroom door, the smell of coffee surprised him.

Padding down the hall, he wondered why Libby was up already.

She was sitting at the table, her fingers cradling a mug of coffee.

"Morning," he greeted, stifling a yawn. "You feeling okay?"

"Bad dream." She lifted the mug to her lips.

His dream had been bad, too. Very bad. But he suspected it wasn't the same kind of bad of which Libby was speaking.

"Want to talk about it?" His back was to her as he pulled a mug from the cabinet and picked up the coffee-pot.

Exhaustion was expressed in her heavy sigh. "A train was coming and I was standing right in the middle of the tracks. Dad was there, too. Behind me. And I knew I couldn't save him."

Something in her soulful inhalation had him turning to face her. Even in the dim, rosy light of predawn, he could see tears gathering in her eyes.

"The worse thing about it was, Dad knew I couldn't save him, too. He wanted to step off the tracks. But he didn't. He gripped my arm and held on to me for dear life. He kept saying, over and over, 'Don't you think we ought to get off the tracks?'"

The need to be near her propelled him forward. Rafe went to the table, pulled out a chair and sat down. "Wonder what brought that on."

"I don't know. Probably something stupid. Something...stupid."

These bouts of vulnerability she suffered pulled at the very deepest part of his emotional being.

"Sounds as though you're talking about a particular something stupid."

Her jaw worked. Then she blurted, "Why would the senior partner of my firm offer to send me help? It's a huge office. I've only met the man a couple of times at the annual Christmas party. He barely knows me. Why would he think I can't handle this? Why can't anyone have any faith in me?''

Rafe set his coffee aside. Quietly he asked, ''Why do you automatically assume that the offer means the man has no faith in you?''

He knew there was more to this than merely an offer of help from her boss in San Francisco. Libby's father was the one standing on those tracks in her dream, not some senior partner. Rafe knew her doubts were caused more by what she thought her father was feeling than by anything else.

Her nightmare might have blossomed due to the offer of help, but the core of her doubt was rooted in David's opinion. It wasn't Rafe's place to reveal David's fear. But he could offer Libby another angle from which to view the offer she'd received via Susanna from her boss.

''It could be that this Mr. Adams wants you to have all the help you need.''

''Why would he think I need help?''

He chuckled then. ''Libby, honey, we all need help. His offer does not necessarily mean he thinks you're incompetent. It could be just what it sounds like—a friendly offer of help.''

The urge to touch her, hug her, pull her tight to his chest, was strong. But he didn't.

In these past days he'd slowly been coming to the conclusion that he'd lost his heart to this woman. She was everything a man could want. Everything a man could need. She was beautiful. Soft and yielding. Strong when she needed to be. And intelligent, too.

She was sweet and wonderful.

A chill crawled across his skin. Yes, she *was* sweet

and wonderful. She was deserving of happily ever after. And Rafe couldn't give her that.

But there was something he could give her. Something she needed. Badly.

"Listen," he told her, "how about if we cook up some of your Dad's favorite foods and take him lunch today? Have ourselves a nice visit."

A hug would do her wonders, he knew. And since he couldn't give it to her, he'd take her to someone who could.

"But will the guards allow us to take food in there?"

"Just let 'em try to stop us."

Her face cleared then, and she smiled. And Rafe felt as if the sun had risen up and flooded the whole darned room with bright, warm light.

Fifteen

When her father reached for his third piece of fried chicken and a second biscuit, Libby smiled. The handmade clay pots in Rafe's kitchen worked perfectly for keeping the hot food hot and the cold food cold.

"Libby, Libby, Libby." David groaned with epicurean pleasure. "These green beans are delicious."

"Sautéed in olive oil and garlic," she said proudly. "Just like Mom used to make."

"Yes, but your mom's biscuits weren't this flaky."

"Shhh." Libby shot a glance heavenward. "We wouldn't want her to hear." But pleasure curled the corners of her lips. Contentment settled over her like a warm and loving shawl when she realized that her dad was thoroughly enjoying her efforts.

"The cole slaw's delicious, too." Rafe reached for the bowl of shredded and dressed cabbage. "I was surprised by your secret ingredients." When David looked at him questioningly, Rafe revealed, "A big dollop of sour cream and a teaspoon of sugar."

For a while, they ate in companionable silence. Finally, David set his fork across his plate and dabbed his mouth with a paper napkin.

"I'm stuffed," he proclaimed. "Filled to the gills. Thanks, sweetheart." He covered his daughter's hand with his own. "I haven't eaten this well in weeks."

"You need to thank Rafe. It was all his idea."

David expressed his gratitude, and then beaming at them, asked, "You two spent the entire morning cooking?"

"*I* cooked," Libby told him. "Rafe continued to read through the evidence."

They discussed the case for a bit: Rafe's theory that someone meant to contaminate Crooked Arrow, the paperwork that documented David had visited the Mokee-kittuun Elders to ask for use of their land, the refusal of that request and finally the electronic diary that made David look as if he had some twisted vendetta against Springer.

"But we have a computer expert working 'round the clock now," Libby said to David. "And she's confident that she'll dig up something that will help our cause."

"I sure hope so."

Dejection rounded David's shoulders.

If he again suggested that they consider giving up and pleading guilty to a lesser charge that might be offered, Libby was sure she'd scream in frustration.

"We're going to be okay, Dad," she said in a rush. "I *do* wish you'd believe that."

She hated the jitteriness of insecurity. Yet, she'd wrestled with that anxiety more in the past few weeks than she had during her whole career as a lawyer. She guessed that was because so much was riding on her getting her father out of this horrible predicament.

Her gaze connected with Rafe's, and she could tell he discerned her lack of confidence. The idea of looking weak had her eyes sliding from his.

"David, I think it's time you tell Libby the truth."

Rafe's quiet statement had her head swiveling back toward him. She looked from Rafe to her father and back again.

"The truth?" David sounded truly bewildered.

"I know you didn't want to say anything, but she's been spending far too much time fighting off the discouraging idea that you doubt her ability as a lawyer. That you don't want her representing you."

"*What?*" Now her father looked shocked. He frowned at Libby. "Why would you think a thing like that?"

Speechless, Libby blinked. When she'd confessed her consternation and doubt to Rafe, she had never thought he'd betray her. Seconds ticked by, and still she said nothing.

"*You* have her thinking a thing like that." Rafe balled up a paper napkin and dropped it onto the top of the metal table next to his plate. "I know you haven't meant to." His tone became peculiarly intense as he stressed, "I know you haven't."

Obviously, he was privy to something. Libby curled her spine and relaxed against the back of the cold folding chair.

Then he added, "Several times now you've suggested that Libby accept an offer of a lesser charge if the opposing counsel should propose one. Your daughter has taken those suggestions as your having doubt in her ability to represent you."

The older man's brown eyes expressed myriad emotions: astonishment, dismay, sorrow, regret.

"Oh, Libby." David whispered the words. "My dear, sweet Libby. I didn't realize. I didn't know what I was doing to you."

Libby hadn't realized she'd put her elbow up onto the table, that she'd begun to worry her lower lip with her knuckles.

"Why, then, Dad?" she asked softly. "If you didn't have reservations about my ability…and you're truly innocent of this crime…then why would you want to plead guilty to *any* charge. I don't understand."

David and Rafe exchanged glances, and Libby saw that Rafe was silently encouraging her father. Yes, it was clear Rafe knew something she didn't.

Reaching to take her hand in his, David told his tale of finding evidence of missing DMBE some months ago, of receiving the necklace along with the anonymous threat against Libby if he went public with what he knew, of becoming so fearful for Libby that he destroyed the electronic post he'd received alerting him to the problem.

"Mom's necklace," she breathed. "I thought I had lost it." The idea that someone had been inside her apartment in San Francisco made her shiver.

"Whoever took it—" her father's words grated with emotion "—broke in while you were there." His tone lowered. "While you were sleeping."

Icy fear and disgust solidified in her stomach. "How can you be sure I was at home?"

"The threat…the letter I was sent had a description of your room." A tremor warbled his indrawn breath. "Of the white satin nightgown you were wearing." He shook his head. "I just couldn't stand the idea that you were at risk because of me. I nearly went insane with worry,

Libby. I destroyed the paperwork I found. And the e-mail. Everything. I just wanted the whole incident to go away. I wanted you to be safe.''

''Oh, Daddy.'' She hadn't called him that in years. She squeezed his hand lovingly.

Her father's eyes were soulful. Rafe's gaze was piercing.

''You two believe the missing DMBE back then is connected to the contamination now?'' Libby asked.

''There's no way to be completely sure.'' David rested the fleshy part of his free hand on the table edge.

Rafe said, ''In light of your accident, and the fact that you were attacked at Jake's—''

''But we can't be certain that those were actual attempts against me.'' Libby released her father's hand. ''That driver never even touched my car. It could very well have been an inexperienced kid behind the wheel. The police think so. And if that purse snatcher meant to hurt me…if he meant to stab me, why didn't he just do it?''

''He took a swipe at me,'' Rafe reminded her.

Libby remembered how scared she'd felt when she realized Rafe had been wounded. She also remembered the night of heated passion that had followed.

Pushing the erotic thoughts from her mind, she said, ''I think that man hadn't meant to hurt anyone. I think you surprised him, is all.''

''Then why did you agree to come to the rez?''

She hardly noticed the irritated accusation in his tone. What she focused on was the question. Why had she agreed to move to Crooked Arrow with him if she really hadn't believed she was in danger?

Because you simply wanted to be near him, a small echo breezed though her mind.

Rafe's sharp jawline was taut. Then he sighed. "You believe what you want. I don't want to fight about this. My only intention in bringing this up was to dispel the uncertainties you were having."

"Sweetie—" her father took her hand again "—I'd trust you with my life. You've got to know that. It was fear that made me balk. Fear for your safety and nothing more."

Emotion lodged in her throat, thick and cloying. She didn't want to cry. Tears would make her look pathetic. However, moisture burned the backs of her eyelids. She swallowed.

"I love you, Daddy. And I'm glad you told me."

Later in the parking lot of the jailhouse, Libby opened the trunk so Rafe could load in the box filled with clay pots, dirty dishes and utensils.

He straightened his spine and she closed the trunk with more force than was necessary.

"I guess I should thank you for what you did in there."

Was that humor tugging at the corner of his mouth? The sight ruffled her ire even more. After all he'd done for her, she shouldn't feel irritated with him. But she did.

"Is there anything else you know that I don't know?" Her brows drew together. "You've kept me in the dark about a lot of things, Rafe. And I have to tell you, it's not fair."

His mouth became a straight line, and Libby was struck with the notion that lips so sensual shouldn't ever take on such sternness. She jerked her gaze from his face. Get a grip, she silently chastised herself.

He crossed his arms over his chest. "I explained to you that I hadn't told you about Cheyenne's vision because I didn't feel I could betray my sister's gift. And your father told me his story and asked me to protect you. He also asked me not to frighten you by telling you of the threat he'd received. I was honor bound to remain silent.''

With his arms swinging easily at his sides, he rounded the car, leaving her standing there in the lot.

So that was it? No apologies? No expression of regret?

The man was enough to make a woman want to grind her teeth right down to the gum.

She watched him get into the car, the sunlight glinting on the long, dark river of his hair, and the embers of her anger died. What remained was a knotty mass of emotion.

She'd already come to the conclusion that Rafe was a man full of dense complexities. Solving the maze of who he was, what he thought, why he did the things he did, would take a lifetime, she guessed.

He was attracted to her, that much she knew. Just as she was attracted to him. And they had surrendered to their desires for each other in one unforgettable night of passion. However, Rafe had been quick to tell her that their night together had been a mistake, that a relationship between them was impossible.

Libby had thought she never again wanted to offer her heart to a man. But after getting to know Rafe...

She sighed. You can't give what has been stolen from you. Rafe possessed her heart already, and there was little she could do about that.

He'd brought her to visit her father in order to allay her doubts about herself. And in doing that, he'd brought about a new understanding between herself and her father. Why would he do something so wonderful?

The man was an enigma. A cryptic labyrinth that seemed unfathomable. Filling her with a host of conflicting emotions. Rejecting her cruelly one moment, making her life bright with warmth and confidence the next.

Squaring her shoulders, Libby walked up to the driver's side door, surrendering to the confusion reigning supreme in her brain.

Rafe stepped up onto the porch of the house. The brass plaque beside the front door read Hopechest. The building served as both office and living space for the director of the ranch, his best friend, Blake Fallon.

He hadn't seen Blake in weeks, Rafe suddenly realized. Ever since Libby arrived in town and his life went topsy-turvy. However, Rafe knew that, no matter how long they had been apart, when he saw Blake it would seem as if no time had passed at all. That was how it was with best friends.

The reception area was decorated just so and the fire burning in the hearth invited visitors into the cozy setting. Blake's secretary, Holly Lamb, stood and offered him a warm smile of greeting.

"How are you, Holly?" he asked.

The slender woman's eyes were nearly obscured by the glasses she wore. Her light brown hair was long and straight, her face devoid of makeup. At first glance, a man would dismiss Holly as plain. But her skin had a glow, her features the shape that one would deem classically beautiful. However, Rafe sensed that, for some reason, this woman was hiding her good looks.

Blake had often bragged about how efficient his secretary was. And more than once Rafe had wondered if the charming young woman might be harboring feelings for her boss. Not that she'd ever done anything outwardly telling. It was just a feeling Rafe had.

"I'm just fine," she told him. "How about yourself?"

"I'm great, thanks."

Sorrow oozed up into his chest, burning his throat. If Todd Lamb—Holly's father—was behind the contamination...

"That's good to hear. You here to see Blake?"

"Sure am. Is he busy?"

"Now, you know he's never too busy to see you. Go right on in."

Common courtesy had Rafe rapping his knuckles on the door twice before turning the knob and entering the office.

"Rafe!" Blake's gray eyes shone with pleasure. He rounded his desk and wrapped Rafe in tight bearhug. "How've you been, buddy?"

"Great." He hugged as good as he got.

Over the years Blake and Rafe had been through a lot together. Yes, as teens they had gotten into trouble with the law. But there were things they had shared, dark secrets as well as joys and dreams, that was rich fodder for the deep-rooted brotherly love they felt for each other.

Blake offered Rafe a seat on one end of the bottle-green leather couch and he sat down on one of the two matching wing chairs.

"I came to see how things are going." Rafe settled his elbow on the armrest.

"Things are looking good," Blake told him. "Evacuating everyone was a little hairy, but it's for the best. I've got lots of paperwork to catch up on." He grinned. "But I'm not complaining, believe me."

"It's good of Joe and Meredith to put up the kids. They didn't even hesitate. Just opened their home."

Blake sighed. "They were great. They're getting up there in years, and I was afraid that, after all Meredith has been through, that the kids might get on her nerves.

But she seems happy to have them there. She and Joe seem to be on a constant honeymoon these days.''

The Colton scandal had been all the residents of Prosperino and the surrounding area had talked about for the past year. First, Joe had been wounded at his birthday party. And then it was discovered that Patsy Portman, Meredith Colton's identical twin, had caused her sister to have an auto accident, dropped the unconscious woman off at St. James Clinic and had somehow succeeded in slipping into Meredith's life. For years she'd managed to deceive those around her into believing that she was Meredith. Patsy had reveled in the Colton wealth.

However, when Patsy's plan to murder Joe failed, the sick and twisted web she'd worked so hard to weave had begun to unravel. Meredith—the *real* Meredith—was once again safely ensconced at home, Hacienda de Alegria, with her husband, and the two were acting like young lovers once more.

"That's good to hear," Rafe said. "I'm glad the Colton clan is enjoying a little normalcy."

Blake chuckled. "It has been a wild ride lately."

Just then, Holly entered with a tray bearing a carafe, two cups, cream, sugar and a plate of cookies.

"I thought you two might like a little refreshment," she said.

"Thanks, Holly." To Rafe, he continued, "Operations around here will be getting back to normal soon too. Meanwhile my staff has been a big help."

Blake reached for the carafe and didn't see his secretary's eyes glitter at the compliment.

Rafe got the impression that if Blake asked, Holly would walk barefoot over hot coals. Holly's eyes darted to Rafe's face, then she dipped her chin self-consciously.

"I'll leave you two to talk," she murmured, and then left them, dignity lengthening her spine.

Before Holly had arrived with the tray, Rafe had been about to reveal to his friend his thoughts regarding Todd Lamb and the DMBE dumping. However, he felt unable to do so. Holly had left the door open and he had no idea who might come or go in the reception area. And he sure didn't think it would be wise to disclose his suspicions about Todd Lamb's involvement when the man's daughter might overhear.

He picked up his cup, took a sip from it and then cradled it between his hands. Changing the subject entirely was the best idea for now.

"So tell me what's happening with the kids," he said.

Blake's gray gaze lit up at the mention of the children.

About twenty minutes later his coffee cup was empty, and Rafe leaned over and set it on the tray. "I'd better get back to work. I'm due to meet Libby soon."

His friend's expression went solemn. "How's the investigation going?"

"Well, the opposing attorneys think they have solid evidence. But I'm confident that Libby will shoot it full of holes."

The men made their goodbyes, and Rafe tossed a friendly wave at Holly on his way out the door. As he descended the porch steps, the sound of tires crunching on gravel drew his gaze.

The man cut the engine of his car and stepped out onto the drive.

"Rafe! What a surprise."

Friendly delight sparked in Joe Colton's blue eyes. His smile dazzled. His handshake was strong, despite the fact that he was over sixty years old. He had an arresting aura that commanded respect.

Rafe held the man in high esteem. When Blake and Rafe had gotten themselves arrested, Joe could have taken the police officer's advice and kept the boys apart. But Joe hadn't done that. In fact, Joe had invited Rafe to his home. It was an invitation Rafe hadn't actually accepted. But the fact that it had been extended meant the world to Rafe.

"Good to see you, Joe. How are you? How's Meredith?"

The joy shining the man's gaze was unmistakable.

"Life has never been better for us. Never been better." Then he grinned. "I'm bringing good news."

"Oh?"

For the first time, Rafe noticed the manila envelope in Joe's hand. He waved it gleefully.

"New reports are in. The DMBE levels are continuing to dwindle. We'll have to keep treating the ground water for a while longer, but this is great news for the ranch, for the whole town."

Rafe's spirits lifted. "Blake will be ecstatic when he hears."

"That's why I came personally. I want to see his face." Then Joe said, "Meredith wants to have a party. She plans to invite everyone. Try to boost morale. This crisis has been hard on everyone in Prosperino."

"You can say that again."

Seeming to be hit with a realization, Joe paused, his face registering regret. "I'm sorry all this has landed on David Corbett's head. You're helping his daughter, aren't you?"

"I am, yes." Rafe nodded.

"Well, just know that I'm praying that the real culprit is soon caught."

Clearly, Joe believed in David's innocence. Joe's opinion meant a lot to Rafe. The gratitude he was feeling must have shown on his face.

"Come on now," Joe said. "There was no way I could believe David would do such a thing. While VP of Springer, David has done a great deal for this town. He's helped the Mokee-kittuun, too, hasn't he? I read about the well he was digging."

"Since he was arrested," Rafe told him, "that project has come to a screeching halt."

"You're kidding?"

"I'm not." His voice lowered as he added, "Since Todd Lamb has taken over, lots of things have changed."

Joe shook his head in disbelief.

"Speaking of Todd Lamb..." Rafe let the sentence trail as he cast a quick glance over his shoulder. "I'd like to ask you to do me a favor."

"Anything, Rafe. You know that."

"I'd like you to keep an eye out for Blake."

Interest sharpened Joe's features, but the man waited in patient silence.

"This has got to be kept in strictest confidence. I'm afraid Holly's father might be involved in this."

"But Todd is Springer's new VP."

"Ironic, isn't it?" Rafe gazed off for a second. "Blake doesn't need more trouble right now, but I'm worried about how Holly will react once her father's involvement is uncovered. However, I'd rather you didn't say anything just yet. I don't know how close Holly is to Todd. If the man should get wind that he's a suspect, he might bolt."

Deep gravity etched itself in Joe's forehead. "I understand. You can trust me, Rafe."

"Thanks, Joe."

"And if David needs a character witness, I'm your man. I've known David for many years. And if I thought about it, I could come up with lots of ways he's helped this community.''

Rafe offered the man a smile of appreciation. ''Well, you start thinking about it.''

Sixteen

"**On** the way home from the courthouse," Libby said over dinner, "I stopped to see Susanna."

"Is she making any progress?" Rafe speared a broccoli floweret.

"She says yes. But, of course, I couldn't tell." She chewed around her grin in silence and swallowed. "But one thing is certain: that girl loves her job."

"Any developments at the courthouse today?"

Libby shook her head. "The judge asked when we'd be ready. Opposing counsel is pressing to start jury selection." She inhaled deeply and stretched her neck muscles. "I need more time."

"Did you tell the judge that?"

"I did. But the other side has their arguments ready. I'm sure they're going to lean heavily on that computer journal they found. They have their witnesses lined up. They want to get this ball rolling."

"Well, don't let them push the ball into motion until you know where it's going to roll."

Softly she assured him, "I won't."

He told her about Joe Colton's offer to give testimony as a character witness on David's behalf.

"That's wonderful, Rafe. Joe is well respected around here."

Rafe began cleaning up the dinner dishes. Libby lent a hand.

The keep-away dance they engaged in had become old hat. He carefully remained in his space and she in hers. They avoided touching each other at all costs. If the atmosphere between them wasn't so charged with serious energy, the whole thing would probably be quite funny. But Libby wasn't laughing.

The strain of living in such close proximity, of wanting each other so badly, yet acting as if that attraction was nonexistent had taken its toll. Both of them were feeling the strain. Each and every time they were together the air in the house was heavy. Tense. Vibrating the very molecules they breathed. However, Rafe seemed completely determined to ignore the almost tangible presence of what was between them. And if he could do it, Libby could, too. Deep down inside, though, she wished things were different.

She had something she wanted to ask. But she realized she'd have to ease into her request. As she filled the sink with soapy water, she said, "I stopped someplace else on the way home from court."

On the way home. The phrase had flowed from her as if it had been the most natural thing in the world.

"Oh? Where'd you go?" But before she could answer, he said, "I thought we'd agreed that if I wasn't with you, you would come directly to the ranch. You probably shouldn't even have stopped to see Susanna without me.''

''We did agree. And I'm sorry. But…I just couldn't resist.''

He was bent over, placing the leftover roast beef into the refrigerator. But her hesitation had his back straightening, his gaze pivoting to her face.

''I stopped at the little house on the road into Crooked Arrow,'' she told him. ''You know the one. There are blankets and baskets and pottery displayed for sale.''

''Margo Redfox's shop. Mokee-kittuun artisans pay her a commission for running the place.''

''She's got some beautiful things there.'' Libby nibbled her upper lip. ''She told me her grandson will have his naming ceremony this evening.'' Before she lost her nerve, she asked, ''Do you think we could go?''

He closed the door of the refrigerator, searching her face for several silent seconds. Libby couldn't tell what he was thinking. What if he refused? Worse yet, what if he suggested that their attending the ceremony would be an intrusion?

Finally he said, ''The gathering won't be anything like the Spring Equinox celebration. This is going to be small. Very small. Cheyenne told me about it. She can't be there, but Alex will be. Since Margo's grandson is the only child being named, it won't take more than ten or fifteen minutes.''

''But…'' Her lips went dry and she moistened them. She hoped he didn't think the eagerness she felt—that fairly quivered in her—was silly. ''Do you think it would be okay? If we went, I mean?''

His wide mouth was unsmiling, his gaze unreadable. She wished he'd say something.

''Sure. If you want to go, we'll go.''

A thrill twittered through Libby.

She'd successfully argued with the opposing counsel in front of the judge for more time to prepare for the trial. And she'd discovered today that the computer expert, Susanna, was making progress. These things should have excited her. Yet, Libby was most energized by the opportunity to attend a fifteen-minute ceremony on the reservation. For some odd reason, she didn't feel the least bit ashamed by that.

The fire in the middle of the cave floor was smaller than she expected. But this night, the cavernous room was aglow with what looked like a hundred flickering candles. The same cracks in the ceiling that let in light during the day, allowed the fire to vent and stirred a current of cool air. The flames on the end of each wick danced and threw shadows against the walls, against the faces of those attending the gathering.

This ceremony might be small compared to the tribal gathering she'd attended, but Alex Featherstone was decked out in all his shaman finery. His impressive head-dress flowed nearly to the floor with white feathers. Turquoise beads hung from narrow rawhide strips near the deep hollows of his cheeks. Time had wrinkled his skin, turned it tough as shoe leather. His black eyes reflected the soft, luminous light no matter what direction he turned his head.

The only people present were the little boy's parents, grandparents and a few friends and family members. Maybe a dozen, all told.

Rafe and Libby had slipped into the room before the ceremony had begun. Margo Redfox had offered them a silent greeting in her gentle smile.

The old shaman called the boy to him. With his spine

rod-straight, the child stepped forward. Alex placed his leathery hands on the boy's shoulders, closed his eyes, lifted his face heavenward.

More beautiful words Libby had never heard uttered. She didn't understand the Algonquian dialect, but she suspected Alex was praying. Every head was bowed, every eye closed. Except for hers. She was too fascinated to miss even an instant of what was happening. She was certain The Great One would understand.

Breathless, she experienced what felt like a strong magnetic tide ebb and flow across every inch of her skin. She felt alive, glowing.

When the reverent appeal was complete, Libby nudged Rafe and he dipped his head so she could whisper in his ear.

"This place really is magical."

She sensed his smile. However, when she pulled back and gazed into his face, his mahogany eyes held a piercing, inscrutable expression. Her heart tripped in her chest, and she hoped he didn't think she was being irreverent. She simply couldn't help it. It's exactly how she felt. She truly believed this cave was enchanted.

Without responding, Rafe lifted his chin and watched the ceremony. Embarrassment had Libby hugging her arms across her chest. She should have just kept her mouth shut and paid attention to the scene before her.

"Like a bright star in the night sky directs the weary and uncertain traveler—" the shaman's rich voice reverberated against the walls of the cave "—this child will grow to be a leader of men. Wisdom will be his companion. Strength of character will be his brother. He will guide those who do not know the way. One who has such a tremendous responsibility must have a strong and dependable name."

Pride gleamed in the eyes of the child's parents, and Libby felt her throat swell with emotion when a tear spilled down the mother's cheek.

"From this day forth, this child will be known as Tipaakke Hongiis. Night Star."

Then the old man began to sing. The lyrics and tune were poignant, like invisible fingers reaching far into the soul to pluck at the strings of one's heart. Libby found it difficult to swallow. Her chin quivered. Tears burned her eyes.

There was silence, then everyone began to file out.

"It's over?"

Rafe nodded. "I told you there wasn't much to it. That the ceremony would be short and sweet."

How could he say that? she wondered. Wasn't much to it? Yes, the ritual had been short. Ah, but the sweetness of it had been breathtaking.

The old shaman had given that child a purpose in life. Alex had offered that boy hope. A noble goal to reach for and attain. The child's parents had seen that and reacted to it with pure loving emotion.

A chilly breeze blew off the ocean, and even though they were more than a mile from the Pacific, Libby could smell the salty tang as they trudged home.

"Fog is moving in," Rafe said.

For several minutes, they walked in silence. The sky was overcast. The air cool. Libby turned up the collar of her jacket.

"Rafe?"

"Hmmm?"

"What predictions did the shaman make about you? During your naming ceremony, I mean. Why did he give you the name Dark Wind?"

She heard him inhale, sensed his chest expand. Then he blew out the breath between parted lips.

"I don't remember his actual words," he began. "I was too young. But many times my mother talked to me about it."

His whole body seemed to tense.

"Every time something bad happened to us, she would remind me of what Alex said on the night of my naming."

Although her eyes were narrowed on the dim ground in front of each step she took, her ears—and her heart— were sharply focused on Rafe's story.

"Darkness is like a protective blanket that shields, she'd tell me. And the wind that blows brings change. Alex apparently assured me and my parents that, in the light of day, better things were to come."

Libby frowned. "It sounds like some sort of cryptic message." What she couldn't bring herself to say was that the motive behind Rafe's name didn't seem to have the same uplifting message as what the shaman had given tonight.

"Your mother reminded you of Alex's message when things were bad," she said. "Tell me. In the light of day, did the wind blow in better things?"

"I can't answer that."

She looked up at him then, but the night obscured his features. A strange sadness seemed to pulsate from him.

"I can't because…" His voice grew hushed. "I'm still waiting for the sun to rise."

Her heart ached, hating the thought that Rafe felt he was living in the dark. Oh, how she would love to help him enter into the daylight. But if he wouldn't talk to her, wouldn't allow himself to get close to her, she simply didn't know how to help him.

Emotion burned her throat and she found it difficult to talk. But she forced herself to reach out and touch his arm.

"Thanks for taking me tonight. It was wonderful."

He must have heard the warble in her tone for he placed his arm around her shoulders. Snuggled in his warm embrace, Libby felt the night wind cool the trails of her tears.

"Come on now," he said softly. "I saw you welling up back there in the cave. It's okay." He grinned. "All women get emotional at naming ceremonies. They think of the children they've had or the children they're going to have. Before you know it, every female nearby is crying like a forlorn mama wolf."

So, he thought she was weeping because of the ceremony they had attended. Well, the gathering had stirred her emotions. But she wasn't crying for that little boy who had received a Mokee-kittuun name tonight. And she wasn't crying—as Rafe suggested—over the children she might one day birth. She was crying for Rafe. And for whatever dark wind soughed through his memories.

"I know just what we need."

His tone took on a false jocularity and she knew he was attempting to lighten her mood.

"How does a mug of mulled wine sound? It'll warm us up and calm you down."

She chuckled. "Mulled wine sounds delicious."

Later, they sat in front of the fire, both of them cradling mugs of warm and spicy wine. The fire in the hearth sizzled and popped as flames feasted on wood. Libby felt haloed in a rosy glow. Several different things were responsible for the feeling, she was sure. The wine, for one. Another was due to the wonderment of the ritual she'd witnessed earlier. And the other was Rafe.

Her tears had affected him. Since they had arrived home, he'd been so gentle with her. So protective.

Darkness is like a protective blanket that shields.

Libby remembered commenting that Rafe's Mokee-kittuun name was a little gloomy. But now that she thought about it, maybe Alex's premonition regarding Rafe's future hadn't been so far off the mark. He was a protector.

Her protector.

"I saw Holly Lamb today," Rafe said.

"Todd's daughter?"

"Umm-hmm. I went to visit Blake at the ranch. Holly works as his secretary." A chuckle vibrated deep in his chest. "I got the distinct feeling that something is there."

He grinned, and warmth curled all the way to Libby's toes.

"A spark," he continued. "Or something between the two of them. Blake and Holly. But the funny thing is, it's clear that Blake doesn't have a clue."

"Men can be quite thick when it comes to matters of the heart."

Their gazes locked. She hadn't meant to get personal; however, apparently she had. Nevertheless, Rafe remained stubbornly silent.

"I was going to warn Blake," he said. "Regarding our suspicions about Todd Lamb."

Her eyes widened. "You didn't, though, right? That would be a terrible mistake."

Dark clouds gathered in Rafe's brown eyes. "Holly's going to need help in dealing with this mess when the truth about her father is revealed."

"But what if she tells her father? He could leave town. He could leave the country." She set her mug on the coffee table and stood up. "You didn't say anything, did you?"

"Not to Blake. I didn't get the chance to." Setting his mug on the end table, he admitted, "But I did tell Joe."

"My God," she breathed. "Of all the stupid things to do. Now Joe Colton knows that we suspect Todd Lamb of the DMBE dumping. I don't get it. You told Joe, but you refused to go to the police with our suspicions."

Rafe stood now and moved closer to her. She felt dwarfed by him. But she'd be damned before she backed down.

"I don't trust the police. But I trust Joe implicitly. And I told Joe he shouldn't say anything just yet."

Their voices raised with each response.

"But he might tell Blake and you just said there's something between Blake and Holly. What if he tells her?"

"Joe won't say anything," Rafe said. "He'll respect my wishes. I have no doubt about that."

"But what if Joe doesn't respect your wishes?" Fury had the words rolling from her before she had time to even contemplate what she was saying. "What if he tells Blake? What if Blake already told Holly? What if Holly is with her father right this very minute? It was a stupid thing to do, Rafe. A stupid thing."

"Don't do that."

"Don't do what? Tell you the truth? Someone has to." Then she repeated, "It was a stupid thing to do."

He swooped toward her and was in her face before she had time to draw a breath.

"I'll tell you what's stupid." The words sounded like the growling of a hungry panther. His fingers bit into her upper arms. "The fact that I can't conquer this need."

His mouth angled down over hers, hard and vicious.

He meant to be cruel. He meant to be brutal. She knew it. But the only result of his kiss was that every devilish craving in her was released.

Her desire for him rushed to the surface, welling, disgorging, and Libby slid her hands around his neck. She reveled in the scent of him. In the spicy, heady taste of him. In the hard mass of him.

He nipped at her bottom lip, and blood swam in her head, dizzying and giddy. He thrust his tongue, deep and plundering into her mouth. But rather than recoil from the harshness of it, she gently sucked. His groan only fueled the fire burning in her. In them both.

She didn't know how, but the buttons of her blouse came undone, his hot hands roving over the lacy fabric of her bra, his lips and tongue tasting the flesh high on her breasts. She pressed a kiss to the crown of his head. Libby dragged frayed and jagged breaths into her lungs through parted lips, feeling smothered, deprived of oxygen. His hands kneaded her breasts, his thumbs roved over her nipples. His touch was rapturous, and her thoughts whirled, her desire burned, raging out of control. Shrugging her arms out of the sleeves, she let the fabric fall, unheeded.

His hair brushed against her shoulders, her chest, her arms. Not letting the filmy buffer of her bra deter him, he took her nipple between his lips and suckled right through the lacy fabric. Libby's body came alive. Arching her spine, she offered him more. And he took it. His hot, moist kisses scalded a trail up her neck, then he ravaged her mouth once more.

He slid his hands up her back, pulling her tight against him. There was no mistaking the hardness of his desire pressing low against her belly, and this set off a chain reaction in her. Her heartbeat hammered. Her blood whooshed through her ears. The desire pulsing through her electrified every nerve ending in her body.

"Oh, Rafe," she whispered helplessly. "I love you."

Those words were like the shock of cold water splashed on hot skin. Her eyes went wide. And then she blinked.

Rafe's head remained buried in the curve of her neck. Her breast filled one of his palms. His other hand tangled deep into her hair. His teeth raked against her flesh, and Libby teetered on the very edge of sanity.

Evidently he hadn't heard her profession. He pulled away from her, straightening his spine until she was forced to look up into his face.

Passion clouded his mahogany gaze. He looked drunk with it. Drugged. And for an instant, Libby wondered if he even knew who she was.

He reached up and cupped his hands on either side of her face. But when he moved toward her, a spark of fear flashed in her gut.

She planted her palm on his chest. "No. No, Rafe."

Her words did nothing to stop him. And his mouth crushed against hers.

Libby struggled, pushing at him, attempting to wriggle out of his embrace.

"No. No!"

From the first day she'd met this man, she'd felt utterly safe with him, protected. But not now. Now she was besieged by pure panic.

As if awaking from some stupefied sleep, Rafe lifted his head and studied her face.

"I don't want this," she rushed to say. "Not like this, Rafe."

A deep frown scored his forehead. And as his eyes

cleared, his expression became more and more disconcerted.

He stepped away from her, his eyes scanning her from head to foot. Standing before him, without her blouse, she felt nude. She didn't fight the need to cover herself. Instead, she lifted her arms and crossed them over her chest, acutely aware of her rock-hard nipples, the now clammy dampness of the fabric of her bra.

As the silent moments passed, Rafe became more agitated. Horrified, even. Finally, he whispered, "What the hell have I done?"

The question wasn't for her. Libby knew that and didn't try to answer. Her own mind was spinning. For the life of her, she couldn't fathom how a simple argument could have escalated into this...frenzy. It was frightening. How had they lost control to this degree?

Maybe because, all along, their power over the passions raging inside them had only been tenuous at best.

Libby hadn't realized she'd been staring at the fire until sudden movement caught her attention. Rafe had bolted for the front door.

"Rafe! Wait!" She reached for her blouse, fumbled to cover herself with it, fastening the one button located between her breasts. Then she raced across the room.

The fog was like a heavy velvet curtain, cloaking everything that lay beyond the front porch. The night air wasn't just chilly anymore, it was biting. And she worried that Rafe had left the house without a jacket.

"Rafe." The thick moisture muted her voice. She called again.

But all she heard was silence, and then the muffled sound of horse hooves fading as he rode away from the house. Away from her.

Seventeen

She came awake slowly, not realizing at first where she was. Feeling the heat radiating from the embers dying in the hearth, seeing the dim glow of the lamp on the table, she remembered she'd been waiting for Rafe to return. She must have fallen asleep on the couch. The clock on the mantel told her it was nearing three-thirty in the morning.

Groggy, she sat up and was startled to find Rafe sitting in the chair, staring at her, his dark eyes expressing a mysterious concentration. Once she was over the surprise of seeing him there, she was flooded with relief that he was home, safe and sound.

"Are you okay?" she asked him.

After he had thundered off into the cold night, Libby had replayed their argument in her head. And she'd continued to rewind her thoughts, going over and over their angry banter, until she realized she kept stopping at the same crucial point.

She'd called his actions stupid. That was what had sparked the anger between them. Before that, it had simply been a discussion.

She certainly hadn't been insinuating that he was unintelligent. She'd only meant to convey that she thought his revealing their suspicions regarding Todd Lamb had been a mistake. However, Rafe had zeroed in on one word. And he'd reacted to it.

Stupid.

Evidently, he'd somehow gotten the notion that she thought he was brainless or dull-witted. Worse yet, he'd acted as if she'd sewn that opinion into some sort of woolen cape and draped it securely around his shoulders.

It had been that one word—stupid—that had caused their argument to spiral out of control the way it had.

As the long hours had passed and she'd huddled on the couch, she'd remembered back to the very first time she'd met Rafe. How he'd remarked on the color of her eyes. Startling had been the word he'd used. And she remembered the anger that had flared in her—not because Rafe had complimented her, but because he'd unwittingly chosen the same descriptive word that Stephen had so often used to lull her into a false sense of security so he could exploit her so ruthlessly.

Just as Rafe's innocent utterance had triggered a response in her—a response prompted from her experiences in the past—so had her remark provoked a reaction from him.

Absently she smoothed a palm over the wrinkles of her blouse.

"I'm sorry, she said. "I'm really sorry."

Although she hadn't thought it possible, his sharp features tightened even more. His dark eyes glistened with sudden emotion. He blinked. Looked away. Lifted a fist and pressed it firmly against his closed eyelids. His sigh was shaky, saturated with emotion.

"You've done nothing to be sorry about," he told her. Moisture still glittered in his gaze, clumping his long, dark lashes, yet not a single tear fell. "It is I who owe you an apology. And I hope I can make you understand me well enough so that you'll accept it."

"Rafe, I—"

"No, Libby," he interrupted. "Don't say anything. Just listen to me."

It was then she noticed that something rested across his lap. A book… A photo album.

"I'm ready to admit it," he said. "I'm finally ready to acknowledge that there's something between us. And I'm not just talking about the physical attraction that keeps taunting us. What's between us is deep. Meaningful." He nodded slowly. "And I'm tired of trying to act as if it isn't there."

As if it had sprouted strong, swift wings, her heart soared. Had he heard her profession of love? She wished she had the nerve to ask. Her pulse palpitated with budding promise about where this conversation was leading.

"I've already said I can't get involved," he continued. "But now, seeing what I nearly did to you tonight, I'm ready to explain to you the reasons why a relationship between us is impossible."

Her hopes plummeted. He had told her early on that he didn't want to become involved. At the time she'd been glad to hear it, because she'd felt the same way. But she'd lost her heart to him—and that had changed everything.

However, her immediate concern was the guilt he obviously suffered over what had happened between them before he left the house. She felt compelled to respond.

"We didn't do anything I didn't want to do. I'm just as responsible for what happened as you are."

She'd wanted his kiss, his touch.

"Don't, Libby. Don't try to make me feel better about this. It isn't going to work."

He hesitated, his gaze burrowing down to her bones.

"I got angry," he said. "And I let that anger become all mangled up with the attraction I feel for you. It was wrong. I shouldn't have let that happen."

Softly she said, "But I provoked you."

"Damn it." His tone was quiet, controlled. His jaw clenched. "You sound just like Onna. That's exactly what she said every time Curtis James decided to make himself feel like a big man at our expense."

He stared into the glowing embers for a moment. Then he said, "Libby, nothing—and I mean *nothing*—you could ever say or do should cause me to lose control. My behavior was deplorable. And I won't allow you to excuse it."

She remembered the dazed look in his gaze when he'd kissed her and fondled her so roughly. She remembered the fear that shot through her. Libby's chin dipped. She felt ashamed that she had been about to disregard her own feelings of well-being in order to assuage his guilt.

Never before had she been willing to disrespect herself. When she'd discovered that Stephen had been married, she hadn't hesitated in booting him out of her life. Why, now, would she ignore her own self-worth when she had clearly seen that Rafe's motivation for passion hadn't been as pure as her own?

"Here." He handed over the photo album that had been resting on his knees. "I want you to see this."

"She's beautiful."

The old black-and-white photo had yellowed with age. The Native American woman had dark, deep-set eyes. Her black hair was long and flowing. Her cheekbones were high, her nose regal, her mouth full. The baby she cradled in her arms was dark-eyed as well.

"That's me she's holding." Reaching over, he fiddled with the stiff pages. "I want you to see her just before she died." He flipped two pages on the large wire rings.

Libby stifled a gasp. Surely, this hollow-eyed, haunted-looking woman wasn't Lorna Running Deer. Her hair was gray at the temples and she looked thinner, almost gaunt.

"That's what living with Curtis James did to my Onna."

Glancing up at his face, Libby saw his eyes had frozen to chips of ice.

"I tried my best to protect her from him. I did."

She felt as if her heart was melting right behind her ribcage.

"When we moved to Prosperino so that Onna could clean Curtis James's house, I was starving for affection. I had lost my father. And I was looking for someone to…I don't know. Give me some attention. Curtis looked at me from the first day we entered his home as if I was something nasty he'd stepped in. Something he couldn't wait to scrape off his boot." Rafe scratched his jaw. "Onna would tell me not to get in his way. That she needed the job to provide for us.

"When she came to me and told me she had a baby growing inside her, and that she was marrying Curtis James, I felt physically ill. Yet at the same time, I was eager for the baby to arrive. Excited about having a baby brother or sister."

As he spoke, Libby perused the pictures in the album. She saw Lorna posed with another newborn. Rafe's brother, River, she surmised. The boy standing several feet from Lorna looked to be about five. Rafe. Unsmiling. Forlorn.

"Curtis adopted me. And when those papers arrived in the mail stripping me of the name Running Deer, I thought sure I'd die. Onna was so happy, though. She thought we'd be a family. But Curtis had no intention of being a father to some half-raised heathen who, in his estimation, had been spared the rod too many times. I honestly believe he adopted me because then, he thought, he couldn't get into trouble for doling out what he called discipline."

His hand lifted in the air and Libby saw that he was shaking.

"I tried hard to be happy. For Onna's sake. But I soon realized that having a sibling only meant more responsibility for me. More worry. You see, Curtis James liked his liquor. And when he got drunk, he teased and taunted the people around him." Absently Rafe scratched his forehead at the hairline. "The man was heartless. Cruel and violent. He abused all of us physically, psychologically, emotionally." His gaze locked onto hers as he admitted, "I learned early on how to take the brunt of that abuse on myself."

Sitting there listening to Rafe's horrible story and not reaching out to him was the hardest thing Libby had ever done.

"I remember once when River was just able to sit up on his own—he couldn't even walk yet—he'd dropped his bottle and milk had dripped onto the carpet. I thought Curtis was going to raise the roof, he yelled so loudly. He'd smacked my mother, and I knew he would be going for River. So I grabbed his cup of hot coffee and spilled it down his leg. On purpose, of course. The beating I got kept me in bed for two days. But the incident had a positive outcome. Curtis stayed sober for nearly a week.'' He swallowed. ''I have dozens of those stories locked in my brain. Dozens.''

Darkness is like a protective blanket that shields. Had Alex Featherstone had some otherworldly knowledge of Rafe's purpose in life when he'd said those words, gifted him with that name? Had he known Rafe would turn out to be a protector of those he loved?

Finally Libby could keep silent no longer. ''Why would she stay with him? Why did she put her children in such danger?''

''Come on,'' he said, his tone harsh. ''It wasn't her fault. This happened thirty years ago, Libby. Where could she go? Where could she work? She felt lucky that Curtis hired her to clean for him. And she felt terribly grateful to him for marrying her once he'd made her pregnant. She was stuck. She had no other alternatives. At least, in her mind she didn't.

''Oh, she tried to protect us, but she was just no match for Curtis. But me...'' His chuckle was humorless. ''I was devious. I found out real quick that it was simple to outsmart my stepfather. Becoming the scapegoat was easy. All I had to do was look for ripe opportunities to make that drunken bum angry. Stupid, he'd call me. Stupid became my nickname for a very long time.''

Her blood froze to slush. Now she understood his angry reaction.

Rafe sighed. ''Onna got sick while she was pregnant with Cheyenne. She died bringing my sister into the world.'' His tone became sharp as steel. ''Onna was in the ground less than a day before Curtis James dropped me and Cheyenne off at Crooked Arrow. Like we were some kind of refuse he didn't want to be associated with. He took River with him, though. And I worried about my brother for years." He pinched at his chin, once, twice. "Curtis died eventually. Cirrhosis of the liver. It was an easy way out for the bastard, if you ask me. And I was able to see River again when he was placed at Hopechest Ranch."

Libby reached over and touched his forearm, but he withdrew from her, and she felt as if she'd been stung.

"Don't, Libby. Don't try to console me. That's not why I told you all this. I want you to understand...I *need* you to understand that all that I went through had an effect on me. My heart is hard. It's like granite. I've got walls built up. Barricades I hide behind. I'm no good for you, Libby. No matter what I feel for you. I can't give you what you need, what you deserve."

Tenderness swelled in her heart. He didn't mention the word love, but he had implied that he felt *something* for her. It pained her to think that she'd come so close to finding the love of her life only to have him turn away from her.

"There are people who can help you, Rafe. People who would make you understand all the anger you feel. Manage it. Channel it into something productive."

He shook his head. "No one can help me. I've been living with this for too long. What's inside me is like calloused skin. It's there to protect. And it isn't going away. Ever." His dark eyes narrowed. "You need to re-alize that."

Rafe stood up then and walked away from her. She heard his steps retreat down the hallway. She heard his bedroom door close.

And Libby had never felt more shut out.

* * *

The next morning after his meditation, Rafe entered the house and was surprised to see Libby's suitcase sitting by the front door. She entered the living room from the hallway, fastening an earring to her earlobe. His pulse thudded dully, and his groin tightened with desire. He knew he'd never live to see a day when he didn't react to her in this manner. Although it was very early, she was dressed for a day at court.

"What's going on?" he asked.

"I'm leaving."

For good, the finality in her tone filled in for him.

"Don't be foolish, Libby. You can't do that."

She planted her hand on her hip. "I'm not going to argue with you. I can't stay here. I can't work here. There are too many...distractions. The judge and opposing counsel are pressing me. I've got to get myself together. Nailing down my case strategy should be my only focus right now. Dad's future depends on how well I do that." She was quiet a moment, and then she added, "I can't do that here."

When she turned and headed toward the kitchen, he followed her.

"This is about last night—"

Libby whirled on him. "Of course it's about last night. It's also about every single moment since I've been here."

The tension. The sensual energy that had plagued them. The desire they had both tried to suppress. That's what she was talking about.

"I'm sorry I can't be what you need me to be," he said. "I'm sorry—"

"What bothers me," she cut him off, "is that you don't feel I'm worth the effort to try."

Rafe clamped his mouth shut. He didn't think she wasn't worth the effort. *He* wasn't worth the effort.

"You've made yourself quite clear," she continued. "There will be nothing between you and me, save our working relationship." She shook her head. "I only wish I was as strong as you. I wish I could tell my heart what to feel. I sure tried. After being so hurt and so disappointed by Stephen, I thought I'd completely given up on relationships. But then you stepped into my life."

Her striking aquamarine eyes expressed utter disillusionment.

She said, "It's just not fair. It's not fair that, knowing how I feel—knowing you feel it, too—you expect me to disregard what my heart is saying." She sighed. Then her tone turned cool. "I'll be at my father's if you need me. If you come up with anything, talk with anyone who can help our case, you can call me there."

"What about the safety issue?"

Her gaze leveled on his. "I want you to know I gave that a lot of thought through the night. I'm not leaving here all flustered and agitated. I really have thought it through. I've decided, and you have to agree, that there hasn't been anything that's happened to me that can honestly be called personally threatening. Because of my involvement with this case, I mean. The car accident was probably just that. And my attacker simply wanted the money in my purse."

"But what about your father's story? The threat against you...the necklace?"

"Rafe, do you have one shred of proof that the two incidents are connected?"

He could only remain silent.

"I didn't think so." She turned and looked at the kitchen counter. "I'll pick up coffee in town." Then she walked past him, back toward the living room. "I'll be at the courthouse all day. And tonight I'll be at my father's."

That was all she said before the front door closed and Rafe was surrounded by quiet.

It was rare that his thoughts were anything but calm, but the chaotic notions swimming in his head made him want to shout. He felt her leaving here was a mistake. That she was putting herself in danger. But he also had to admit that his emotions were involved in the forming of those opinions.

She had a point. The two incidents she was involved in could be explained away as having absolutely nothing to do with the legal mess her father was in. And there wasn't a bit of evidence to connect the current DMBE contamination with the e-mail David had received months ago.

This was what happened, Rafe realized, when a man let his feelings get all tangled up with reality. It was too easy to see things that weren't there. Too easy to twist facts into something they weren't. Maybe Libby was right. Their being apart was for the best. For them, personally. And so that they could better focus on building David's case.

Silently he chanted, This is for the best.

And he was going to try like hell to make himself believe it.

Eighteen

His world had made a dramatic change in the last week. Normally, Rafe thought of himself as a clear thinker with a calm and steady spirit. But since Libby had moved out of his house, his life seemed empty. His thoughts and his soul were constantly haunted by the sweet memories; the night of passion they had shared, the long talks they'd had, the sight of her dancing around a blazing bonfire, the poignancy shining in her gorgeous gem-colored eyes as the young boy had received his Mokee-kittuun name.

Inside the walls of his home, the quiet that he'd once found so soothing now drove him nearly insane. Sleep had become a mischievous child bent on playing a taunting game of hide and seek. Without Libby's vibrant energy, his house was desolate. And Rafe had taken to driving the streets seeking escape.

He'd seen her once over the last several days, talked to her twice over the phone. Both times he'd reported on people he'd interviewed. And both times the awkwardness, crackling with static, triggered a clipped and recognizably shielded tone in her voice.

This was for the best, he kept telling himself. His mind believed this command just fine. He only wished he could get his heart to obey.

As he drove along Prosperino's main thoroughfare, he saw Margo Redfox exit a shop. One arm clutched a large package of purchases and the other grasped the hand of her young grandson. Rafe smiled and lifted a hand in greeting. When Margo tipped her chin to return the salutation, her toe caught a high spot on the pavement and she went down onto her knees. The groceries she'd been carrying scattered across the sidewalk.

Immediately, Rafe pulled his truck to the curb. The sound of the child's cries floated on the air. Rafe cut the engine, his eyes never leaving Margo. It was then that he saw an extraordinary sight.

Todd Lamb came out of the post office and walked right past the fallen woman and her grandson, right past all the groceries that had tumbled from her bag. He actually kicked a banana out of his path as he strode by.

Rafe rushed to Margo.

"How clumsy of me," she told him. "I'm okay." She gathered her grandson up in a comforting embrace. "Everything is okay," she crooned to the boy. "I am fine. You are fine."

Anger roiled in him as he watched Todd's retreating back. Rafe gathered up a can of coffee, a quart of milk, three oranges. When he went to fetch the now bruised banana, Rafe moved right on past the piece of fruit and jogged to catch up with Todd.

His hand clamped down on the man's shoulder. "Hey, man, what the hell's the matter with you?"

Lamb turned around. Rafe had never been this close to the man before, and he noticed that his green eyes were flecked with brown. A frown wrinkled Lamb's brow, his gaze registered a conglomeration of irritation and surprise.

"I beg your pardon?" he asked, deftly shifting from Rafe's grasp.

Rafe was taken aback. Lamb didn't seem the least bit affected by his anger.

"Why didn't you offer the lady a hand?"

Without hesitation, Lamb responded, "What lady? What are you talking about?"

Anger turned to rage as Rafe realized that Lamb hadn't offered to help Margo Redfox because he hadn't even seen the woman. She was Mokee-kittuun. And because of that, he hadn't been aware of her existence on the street!

Then Lamb seemed to actually see Rafe for the first time since being approached. Denigration flattened the man's gaze.

In that moment, Rafe's all-consuming goal was to force Lamb to recognize him as a human being—as a man. And knocking Todd Lamb on his ass right here on Main Street with a well-placed punch square in his face would do just that.

His fist balled as he simultaneously murmured a filthy expletive that thoroughly insulted Lamb's mother.

"Rafe!"

Libby's shout nearly failed to penetrate the fog of Rafe's fury. But the sound of her high heels clipping across the asphalt street caused some of the tension in his shoulders to ease. He relaxed his hand, blinked, turned to watch her step up onto the curb.

"I've been looking everywhere for you," she said.

Her tone sounded breathless and contained a false cheeriness. It was clear she was purposefully avoiding the ugly scene that had swiftly been developing between himself and Lamb.

"I've got good news." She grasped his forearm, firmly steering him around, completely ignoring the older man. "Let me tell you all about it."

They took several steps toward Margo Redfox. Libby whispered, "What are you doing?"

"The man's a jackass," Rafe told her. "I was about to teach him some manners."

She hustled him along the sidewalk. "Let's go help Margo gather her things."

By this time the Native American woman had calmed her grandson and was just putting the last of her groceries into the bag.

"I'm really okay, Rafe," Margo said. "Thanks for stopping to help."

He nodded, and Margo bid both Rafe and Libby good-bye.

Rafe knew Libby's gaze had settled on him, and at the same time the air around them seemed to constrict.

"What's the good news?" he asked. "Or were you just making that up to get me away from Lamb?"

A bright smile filled her beautiful face and Rafe felt as if he'd been thrown by a wild Appaloosa.

"I've got good news like you wouldn't believe. Susanna's discovered that the most damaging documents—the pages of the electronic journal—were uploaded onto the Springer's server from a remote location. She found a public IP address buried in the headers of the documents."

"What do you mean, public address?"

"Someone used a computer that has public access.

Like, say, in the local library, or a school or university.''
Excitement fairly sparkled in her gaze. ''Now, this information in itself won't clear Dad. But I've talked to
him about the dates and times that the journal pages were
created and he says some of those days were when he
was in regularly scheduled meetings. I've got to go
through those evidence boxes and find documentation
that verifies Dad's presence in those meetings on-site at
Springer when those uploads were made off-site from the
public IP address. If I can find that, then it'll prove Dad
is innocent since he can't possibly be in two places at
once.''

She shook with anticipation. ''This is Dad's saving
grace, Rafe. This is it. If all goes well, there won't be a
trial at all.''

''Does Susanna believe this info—the public address—
will prove who uploaded the documents?''

Libby's shoulders rounded. ''No. But if we identify
the location of the uploads, then we can check the insti-
tution's records of who used their computers at those
times.'' She refused to be daunted. She grinned. ''We're
close, Rafe. Very close.''

''You need help wading through those boxes of papers?''

She nodded. ''Sure—''

But then she cut herself short. Discomfort crept between them.

Her eyes skittered away from his. ''On second thought,
maybe I should do this on my own.''

This is for the best. The words echoed through his head
like a mantra.

''Whatever you say.'' But Rafe felt as if his heart was
being squeezed in a hot steel clamp and he struggled to
breathe normally.

Her chin tipped up. "There's something you should know." She took her full bottom lip between her teeth hesitantly. Then she said, "I've gone to the police with our suspicions. Kade Lummus knows nearly everything. I spent an evening filling him in. I told him we suspect Crooked Arrow was the target. I told him you overheard Springer executives say that the land must be procured at all costs. I didn't reveal Todd's name. I couldn't bring myself to do that without clear-cut proof. I also told Kade about the tipped aquifer." She added in a rush, "But I didn't say a word about the cave." She paused a moment. "Although I don't want you to be upset, I do think you should know I went to Kade with all this."

So it was Kade now, was it? Something dark and swampy filled Rafe's chest. He knew what it was. Knew he had no right feeling jealous. He said, "Okay, so I know."

Hurt clouded her countenance. Well, she could just join the crowd. He was hurting, too.

"If there's anything else I can do, you let me know." He walked away then. He got into his truck, turned the key in the ignition and started the engine. He drove away.

In the rearview mirror, he watched her watching him. His chest throbbed as if a deep infection had taken root there. Soon David's name would be cleared. Soon Libby would be returning to San Francisco. Soon she'd leave his life forever.

Hopefully, she'd find a man to love her. Give her every good thing she deserved.

And him? Well, he'd have to learn to live with memories. Of touching her. Kissing her. Holding her. Loving her. Those would have to be enough.

Libby heard a thump. She lifted her eyelids, but all she saw was darkness. All she heard was the quiet of midnight. The soft ticking of the grandfather clock. The barking of a neighbor's dog.

Rolling onto her back, she was cognizant of the cotton bed sheets cool against her skin. She lay there wondering if she'd actually been awakened by a noise, or if she'd been dreaming. Silent seconds ticked by. The dog quieted, and finally lulled by a sense of safety, she decided to relax and go back to sleep.

The whisper of shoes on carpet had her eyes opening wide. Movement in the gray shadows caused adrenaline and stark raving fear to surge though her.

Angry hands were on her before she had time to scream.

She tasted the leather of gloves as a hand crushed over her mouth. There was no way she was going down without a fight. She lashed out with a tightly clenched fist, but all she hit was the shade of her bedside lamp, sending it crashing to the floor. With her second attempt, she connected with the midsection of her attacker. The ''Oomph'' she heard was definitely male, as was the sheer strength of him.

Libby tried to kick herself free, but her feet were entangled in the blankets. Cold sweat broke out over her body as she thrashed. She attempted to bite down on the hand at her mouth, but the man was squeezing the hollows of her cheeks, his fingertips biting into her flesh, the pain bringing tears to her eyes. The gloved hand was removed from her mouth.

''N-n-no!'' she said, stricken that the word had come out in such a raspy whisper. Certainly she could do better than that.

But just as she inhaled to shriek, something soft—a damp cloth—was pressed against her face. The cloyingly sweet stench filling her mouth and nostrils made her stomach roll.

Oh, Lord, help her. She was in trouble.

Blackness swirled around the edges of her consciousness, and she pitched headfirst into it.

Nineteen

"**I**'m really not in the mood for company."

"Well, hello to you, too, brother of mine."

Cheyenne smiled sweetly and brushed past him, entering his living room. Jackson remained on the porch, nodding a silent—almost apologetic—greeting. Rafe inched back and let his brother-in-law inside.

"Honey," Jackson said to his wife, "maybe we should come back some other time. It is awfully late."

"Oh, poo." She shooed this suggestion away. "He's up, isn't he? And he's even dressed. It won't kill him to visit with us for a few minutes."

Jackson looked at Rafe. "We were with Alex Featherstone."

"And we drove by on our way home," Cheyenne added. "Saw your lights on and thought we'd stop by."

Rafe grunted. "My house is nowhere near Alex's."

His sister grinned. "Yes, well…let's just say I needed to come see you."

"About what?" His question was sharp.

"My, but you're in a foul mood," she commented.

Jackson wandered off toward the kitchen. "Mind if I have a beer? I'm parched."

"Make yourself at home," Rafe called.

Cheyenne took his hand and led him to the couch. "Come sit down and tell me all about it."

"All about what?"

She shot him a knowing look.

Rafe sighed. "Okay, what have you seen?"

Her shoulders lifted and her dark eyes sparkled with joy. "Not much. But I know you're in love. And I think it's wonderful."

He was silent, not knowing what to say. The fabric of his worn jeans was smooth against his palms. Finally, agitation got the better of him and he rose. He strode to the window.

"Your gift didn't give you enough information." Anger sparked deep in his belly. "There's nothing wonderful about it."

The night looked as bleak as the dark wind blowing through his empty soul. Without turning around, he said, "Why would fate bring a woman into my life that I cannot have? A woman who is too good, too kind, too loving for the likes of me? Cheyenne, if Libby and I were to be together, I'd snuff out her spirit in no time."

His sister was quiet for so long that finally Rafe pivoted to face her. Her eyes were filled with concern.

"No human knows better than fate." Her expression took on a gentle chiding. "Only a man with an awfully high opinion of himself—or an utter fool—would reject a blessing bestowed on him by The Great One."

The muscle in the back of his jaw tensed so tight it hurt. "If this is a blessing," he murmured, "I'd hate to see a curse."

"Stop it, Rafe. Don't make jokes about something this important."

"What's important," he pointed out, "is that everyone comes to understand that I'm no good for Libby. Just like Curtis James was no good for Onna."

Cheyenne sighed. "When are you going to realize that we all have free will? Mother made her choices, Rafe. And who knows? Maybe fate intended for her and my father to get together. Maybe it was the only chance River and I had to come into the world."

He stuffed his hands deep into his pockets. Rafe's faith was great. He truly believed in a Higher Being. He believed that something bigger than himself created the earth and all that was in it. He believed that blessings were gifted, that afflictions were exacted. But when his sister began to talk so esoterically, it made him a bit uncomfortable.

"You can't convince me that Curtis James was Onna's soul mate."

Cheyenne came to him, then. She stood so close that he could smell the smoky sage of the shaman's smudge stick clinging to her clothing.

"Ridge Running Deer was Mother's soul mate. You and I both know that." Then she asked, "Is that what's worrying you? You want to know if Libby is your soul mate?"

Dark gazes collided.

When he didn't speak, she continued, "My gift hasn't told me if Libby is your life partner. But I do know that, if taken to the sacred cave, the woman you will spend forever with will react physically to the magic found there.''

Rafe went utterly still, his heart pounding.

Cheyenne shook her head and chuckled softly. ''At first I thought my vision, my feelings, were somehow confused. I've never thought of the cave in terms of being enchanted or magical. To me it is hallowed ground. But that's exactly what kept coming back to me. Magic. Enchantment.''

His knees wobbled and he didn't trust himself to speak. His mind was racing with the memories of his and Libby's time spent in the cave together. On both occasions, she'd actually broken out in gooseflesh and claimed that magic swirled in the air.

Libby was meant for him. Forever. For always.

He'd felt it deep in his bones. But until this moment, he'd been determined, in his puny human way, to ignore what instinct and his heart were telling him.

However, if The Great Spirit intended for the two of them to be together, who was he to refute the notion? He trembled as joy surged through him. The idea of actually spending his life with the woman who had stolen his heart was utterly overwhelming.

''She is a wonderful person.'' His tone was blistered, parched, and he didn't know if he was speaking to his sister or himself. ''I think she understands me. Knows me better than I know myself. Do you know she suggested that I change my name back to Running Deer?''

''What an amazing idea.'' Cheyenne smiled. ''Living with the James name, day in, day out, just might be part of your problem, brother. You're not a James. Have never been one.''

Yes, but his years as a James had shaped him in some not-so-nice ways. What about the leftover effects of his dysfunctional past? What about the bitterness and anger harbored so deep within him? What about his fears that he might somehow suffocate all those things in Libby that made her such an exquisite person?

Then, Cheyenne's advice came back to him: Only a fool would second-guess fate.

"I know you just got here," Rafe told his sister. As he spoke, he moved toward the closet. "But I need to go out." He pulled a jacket off its hanger. "Like I told Jackson, make yourself at home. Stay as long as you like. Just lock up when you leave."

Cheyenne laughed, evidently sensing his destination without his saying a word. "Don't you worry. We'll do that, brother."

The tree-lined street where Libby grew up was quiet. A dog barked when he got out of his truck, but it was a halfhearted alarm at best.

There was an eagerness in Rafe's step that had him springing up the sidewalk. During the drive here he'd tried several different speeches. Would Libby forgive him for being so stubborn? For pushing her away over and over again?

Yes! resounded through his brain and Rafe grinned. She had to.

He stepped up on the porch, raised his index finger toward the buzzer, and his smile dissolved.

The door was ajar.

For a moment, his mind couldn't seem to grasp the implication. Then utter terror skittered across every inch of his flesh.

With the back of his hand, he pushed open the door. The interior was still as death, dark as a tomb. He swiftly but thoroughly scanned the shadowy recesses of the first-floor rooms. Then he took the stairs two at a time.

Every cell in his body urged him to call out her name. But he kept his lips pressed tightly together. If an intruder was in the house, he didn't want to reveal his presence.

His heart thundered, his blood raced.

As often as he'd worked with Libby in David's house, he'd never been upstairs. Didn't know which room she slept in.

Systematically, he entered the door at the top of the stairs. The scent in the air was faded, but definitely masculine. He snapped on the light. Took in the cherry furniture. Everything in order. He flipped off the light switch and crossed the hall. Bathroom. The third room, another bedroom, was neat and tidy.

He entered the next bedroom, listened to the silence, then felt for the switch. When he turned the light on, fear lumped in his throat. The lamp, having been knocked to the floor, threw garish shadows across the chaotic room. The bedclothes had been dragged halfway to the door. There had obviously been a struggle here.

Training had him warding off the panic that pressed in on him. In automatic mode now, he snapped off the light and went to search the remaining rooms on the second floor.

At the far end of the hallway, he slowed. Dim light glowed from beneath the closed door. Stealthily, he reached for the doorknob, turned it. Like a bolt of lightning, he opened the door and entered the room, ready for whatever awaited him.

A scream ripped through the night. And Susanna Hash jumped up from the chair she'd been perched on. Fear and anger deeply scored her forehead, and she tore the headphones from her ears.

"Rafe, what are you doing? You scared the bejesus out of me!"

"Libby's gone. Her room's a mess."

"What do you mean?" Confusion beat out the young woman's anger.

Impatience flared in Rafe. "She's gone." Then he asked, "What are you doing here?"

"Working. Libby said there was no reason to pay for a hotel when there was plenty of room here."

"When did you see her last?"

Susanna shook her head. "We ate dinner together, then I came up here to work. I took a break around nine. Had a shower, went downstairs for a drink of water. She was going through those boxes down there. Then she tapped on my door about eleven to say good night. I've been working ever since."

He recalled the state of Libby's room. "You didn't hear anything? No scuffling? No screams?" Rafe tried to tame his biting tone, but the claws of panic were tearing into his chest, refusing to be ignored.

"Rafe—" apology whined in the young woman's voice "—I was listening to my music." She offered up the headphones she held in her hand. "Who would come in here?" she demanded. "Who would want to take Libby? I don't get this."

"I don't have time to explain."

His mind churned. What to do. What to do.

He knew Lamb was behind this. Knew it as well as he knew his own name. But he had no clue where Todd Lamb lived. Or where he might take Libby…what he might do to her.

That last thought had dread rising in his throat, burning like acid. He nearly groaned. Calm. Calm. He needed to remain calm or he'd be no good to Libby.

Rafe needed help. But to whom could he turn?

As a kid, the treatment he'd received from the Pros-perino Police Department had been harsh, and he still embraced his bitter feelings about that.

But you were a hooligan back then. A thief. A juvenile delinquent. You deserved the treatment you received.

Well, maybe not all of it…but some of it.

"Get yourself dressed and come downstairs," he told Susanna. "I'm calling for help. I'm sure the police will want to talk to you."

Rafe rushed down the steps, picked up the phone in the study and pressed 911. It took what seemed a lifetime to finally get connected to the police station. The adren-aline and frustration roiling in him had him barking out the name of Sergeant Kade Lummus.

"Well, call him at home," Rafe shouted into the phone. "Tell him to meet me at the station. I'm on my way."

Twenty

"**L**ibby told me that she came to you about our suspicions."

Kade Lummus looked at Rafe. "But she never mentioned Todd Lamb's name."

Rafe said, "Well, now I have. You've got to find him. Send someone to the man's house, Sergeant."

It was all Rafe could do to remain seated.

Evenly the officer said, "I've already asked you to call me Kade." He looked up from the report form he was filling out. "What we both need to do is just calm down. We're not going to get anywhere if we're upset. Can I get you some coffee or something?"

"I don't want any coffee. I want you to find Libby."

Lummus set down his pen. "Rafe, I've got an officer talking to the woman who's staying at the Corbett house. I've got another officer at the jail talking to David about the threat he received against Libby. We want to find her just as much as you do.''

Rafe's frustration level was rising off the charts. ''But Lamb is the key. Get someone to pick the man up!''

''Look.'' Lummus sighed. ''You've got to try to see things from where I'm sitting. We have no evidence that Todd Lamb is guilty of anything. The man could be innocent as a...well—'' he shrugged ''—as a lamb.''

He looked at Rafe, and seeing no response, the officer offered him a silent apology in his embarrassed grimace.

''I can't go banging on his door and accusing him of kidnapping without hard evidence to back up those claims. I've got a patrol car cruising past his house every fifteen minutes. If he's out on the prowl, up to anything at all that even begins to look suspicious, we'll bring him in for questioning. You can bet on it.''

Rafe knew the man was right. But sitting here doing nothing when Libby might be hurt, lying in some gutter bleeding...dying...

He couldn't stand it. He got up and paced the small office like a caged tiger. Every nerve in his body jangled. He'd never forgive himself if he lost her just when he'd finally allowed himself to open his heart to the amazing blessing fate was offering him in her.

Planting his palms on Lummus's desk, he steadied his tone. ''Is there someone else I could talk to? Someone who has the authority to pick Lamb up *now*?''

Kade's eyes narrowed. Quietly he said, ''Sit down and relax. Trust us to do this job right. Trust us to find her.''

He'd offended the man. Rafe sat down on the padded seat of the metal chair.

Trust us...trust us.

Libby had wanted to go to the police from the moment

he'd told her his suspicions about Crooked Arrow being the target for the contamination and Todd Lamb's involvement. But Rafe had talked her out of it.

If he'd been able to trust the authorities, it could be that Lummus would have put Lamb under some kind of surveillance weeks ago, just as he was doing now. Under police scrutiny, Lamb might not have had the freedom to break into Libby's house, to steal her away in the night.

Rafe looked around at the bustling station. Phones rang. Men scrambled. Knots of officers gathered to discuss strategies for searching the town and the surrounding area to locate Libby.

In that instant, Rafe realized that the color of his skin, his high cheekbones, his dark, deep-set eyes, his heritage, even his history of juvenile delinquency hadn't kept the police from believing and acting on his charge that Libby had been kidnapped. As he sat there with noise buzzing around him, he was struck with an amazing revelation. Racism never had been—and never would be—a one-sided issue. He harbored prejudices himself. He was ashamed of the realization, but it was the truth.

Cultivating a trustful spirit wasn't an easy task. Especially when there were so many bigoted and hateful people roaming the earth. People just like Todd Lamb. But Rafe had learned something tonight. He could no longer allow himself to nurture intolerance in his soul. In any form. No matter how others may behave, he would strive to treat his fellow man with the trust, respect and dignity that every human being had the right to expect.

A flurry of movement at the front of the room captured his attention. Upon seeing Jackson and Cheyenne, Rafe rose and strode toward them.

His sister was obviously shaken and distressed.

Jackson spoke first, keeping his voice as calm and low as possible. "Cheyenne had a vision. She had to see you."

"What is it?" Rafe asked her. "What did you see? Is it Libby?"

She nodded, tears spilling from her dark eyes. Rafe felt nauseated. Never had he seen his sister this distraught by a vision.

"I felt pain," Cheyenne said. "Shivered with both cold and fear."

Trepidation solidified in Rafe's stomach until he ached with it.

His sister's dark eyes closed. "There is danger. Terrible danger. And water. Water is rushing. Flowing."

Rafe was aware that Cheyenne had switched from past to present tense. It was almost as if she were in Libby's head, experiencing Libby's reality.

"It's d-dark. Too dark to see. C-cold. Confined." Her tone was raspy as she added, "I'm g-going to die."

Insanity threatened to overthrow his thoughts. But Rafe beat it back. He couldn't help Libby if he let himself get lost in his fear of losing her. He rewound the clues in his mind, trying valiantly to shut out Libby's physical and emotional torment.

Cold. Dark. Rushing water. Confined.

The sacred cave. She was tied up and being held in the cave. His gut told him.

But how could Lamb know about the Mokee-kittuun holy site? It made no sense. However, he had tremendous faith in his sister's gift. He would tell Lummus. Then he would go rescue his woman.

"But I have no jurisdiction on Crooked Arrow," the sergeant said after Rafe had explained. "My men can't

go onto reservation property without permission from the
Mokee-kittuun police. I'll call.''

"You do that.'' Rafe turned and started for the door.

"Wait!'' Kade shouted. "Don't you go out there
alone.''

Rafe ignored the man's advice.

His tires slid in the loose gravel at the foot of the hill
when he brought his pickup to an abrupt halt. The vehicle
had gotten him as close as it could. The rest of the journey would be on foot. He thanked The Great One when
he looked for and found a flashlight in his glove com-
partment.

Rafe kept sweeping his glance in a wide arc. He saw
nothing but rocks, vegetation and shadows. Heard nothing but the wind and the crunch of gravel beneath his
boot heels as he raced along the path.

The question of how Lamb knew about the cave continued to niggle at his mind. Either Libby had told the
man or else Todd was working with someone from the
Mokee-kittuun tribe.

He slipped into the cave and hurried down the passageway as quietly as possible. He hadn't seen a vehicle
at the foot of the hill, but that didn't mean Todd or someone else wasn't there guarding Libby.

Why guard her, a stark voice rose up in his head, if
the intent was to kill her? Remove her from the case?

Dread pained him, shook him to the core.

Entering the chamber, Rafe paused. Listening—feeling—for human presence.

The faint sound of water flowing was all he heard. He
frowned, sensing nothing but a confusing solitude.

"Libby?'' His shout reverberated off rock. He turned

on the light and swept the cave with it. The beam wasn't
strong enough and faded into shadows. Feeling the need
to be completely thorough, he searched the rocky ledges
and crevices of the cave, moving to the far end where
the cascading waterfall drowned out his thoughts and all
he had left in his head was pure panic.

"Where are you, Libby?" he whispered, emotion
swelling, aching in his throat.

He lifted pleading eyes heavenward. "Oh, Great Father, please help me."

Rafe let his lids close and he inhaled deeply, endeav-
oring to focus his mental energy away from the unnerv-
ing terror in him and onto the clues that Cheyenne had
revealed.

Cold. Dark. Rushing water. Confined.

He'd taken the confined to mean she was secured in
some way. Tied with ropes or tape. But what if the description meant something else? What if the place she
was in was confined?

"She's cold," he repeated aloud. "It's dark. There's
water around her. And wherever she is, it's cramped."

Rushing water. He thought of the Pacific tides ebbing
and flowing. Waves pounding the surf.

But confined.

A boat? Could she be in the hull of a boat? Racing
out into the sea where Todd meant to dispose of her
body—

"No!" He raked his fingers through his hair. He
couldn't think like that. "She's alive, damn it!"

Rushing water. Confined.

Flowing water. A cramped space with flowing water.

"The well." The idea passed from his lips on a breath
just as it entered his head. Libby was at the well site that

Springer had been drilling for Crooked Arrow. There was a small sheet metal building there. That had to be it.

He dashed toward the cavern entrance, but paused near the center of the cave. The police were coming here. He had to leave word that she was located in the abandoned well site.

How could he leave a message when he had no paper, no writing utensil?

The beam of his flashlight illuminated the blackened circle where hundreds of fires had burned over the years.

Ash. Charcoal. Could he use it to leave the authorities a message?

"Kit-tan-it-to'wet," Rafe whispered to the most Holy One, "forgive me. I'll come back and clean up the mess." Using his index finger, he printed block letters right there on the floor. As he worked, he continued to pray. "Please grant me the wings of Brother Eagle, the swift feet of my totem, Brother Deer. I must reach Libby in time."

He stood and surveyed his work. Certainly one of the policemen would see the message. He sprinted from the cave.

Large construction equipment, dark and dormant, littered the fenced-in area. Located seemingly out in the middle of nowhere, the abandoned well site was silent. But the chain used to secure the eight-foot-high steel link fence lay on the ground, snipped with metal cutters.

Every nerve in Rafe's body came alive. Leaving his truck just outside the gate, he cautiously approached the sheet metal building that had been temporarily constructed to protect the workers from the weather.

Somewhere on the far side of the makeshift building,

metal flapped in the chilly breeze, clanging against metal. The rusted hinges squeaked like mice as he inched open the door. He slipped inside, flashlight in hand.

What would he do, a forlorn voice echoed in his head, if all he found was the lifeless body of the woman he loved? Immediately, he shoved the question from him.

All Rafe could hope was that Lamb had been unable to actually hurt Libby. That he'd only left her here to freeze to death, or starve.

Hearing nothing but normal night sounds, Rafe snapped on the light and called out Libby's name.

"If you're here, honey," Rafe shouted, pointing the light from one dark crevice to the next, "I need to hear from you. Call out, if you can. Kick something. Knock. Make some noise, honey. Help me find you, Libby."

Moving counterclockwise, he searched the building. Construction debris littered the floor. Rafe was afraid to step on the pieces of sheet metal, fearing Libby just might be hidden beneath one.

Not until he reached the back of the building did his emotions begin to churn. Fear. Doubt. Panic. All of these feelings swirled inside him.

"Help me, Libby." He heard his voice tremble. "You've been smarter than me all along," he called out, lifting a large cardboard box and then tossing it aside. "You've known that this thing between us is special. Even before I begrudgingly admitted it, you knew. You tried to make me see. that. I've been stubborn. Willful. I thought I could fight it. Well, now I know I've been wrong. Terribly wrong. And I need to know you forgive me."

He peered beneath the huge crane. "I'll do anything, honey. I want you to know I'll go see a therapist. I'll talk about the past. I want to let it all go. That will be good, don't you think? And I do want to be a Running Deer again. I do. And I love you for suggesting it.''

This babble helped him to retain his grip on reason.

"You're here, Libby. I know you're here.'' Louder he said, "I love you, woman. Do you hear me? We can't be together if you don't help me find you.''

Finally, his panic welled to the surface like dry volcanic ash, spewing from him in a wretched eruption. *"Libby!"*

The echo of his voice hadn't died before a sound caught his attention. The narrow shaft of light spanned the dark interior. Some slight movement caught his eye. A rope hung down from the topmost reaches of the boom of the crane he'd searched under. The rope quivered just the slightest bit.

Rafe stepped over the metal barricade, then reached down to tug aside the sheet metal that covered the hole in the ground—the actual well that had been dug.

Libby's coppery hair glinted in the dim light thrown by the flashlight.

"Talk to me, honey,'' he coaxed, now shoving the pieces of metal out of the way with renewed energy. "Look up at me, Libby. Show me those beautiful eyes of yours.''

She tipped her chin up then, and the tears streaming from her face both elated him and disturbed him mightily.

She was alive! And he had to get her out of there.

Laying flat on his belly, he reached for her. But she was dangling too far down.

Libby shivered. Her skin was pale as cream and she was filthy.

"I'm going to get you out of there," he softly crooned. "Don't worry."

The gag on her mouth kept her silent, but the pain in her gaze spoke volumes.

Her chin lowered back down to her chest, and Rafe realized how weak she was. The rope bit cruelly into her upper arms. Adrenaline streaming through his body, he shot to his feet, ran to the crane and climbed up into the huge piece of machinery. Shining his light across the console, he saw the ignition. No key.

He scrambled down from the cab.

"Hold on, honey," he said to her. "I'm getting you out of there."

The hole was about four feet across. Straddling the well was awkward. Rafe placed his weight directly overtop Libby. He grabbed the rope and began hoisting her up.

She groaned.

There was no way for him to be gentle. All he could do was get her out.

When he raised her enough to grasp her arms, she let out another painful moan.

"Almost, honey. Almost."

Something down below, deeper in the well, scraped the dirt sides of the hole.

"What was that?" he asked.

The bewilderment in her eyes told him she had no clue.

As gingerly as possible, Rafe pulled Libby to one side, laying her down beside the well. Immediately, she began to squirm her way farther from the gaping hole. Again, they heard a scraping.

"What the hell—"

Rafe heaved on the rope that had been secured to her

ankles. What he saw on the end of it, raised the hairs on his arms and the back of his neck. He went still.

"Libby, don't move."

She relaxed.

"I'm not sure, but it looks like some kind of detonation device."

He wrestled with the cloth that was knotted over her mouth, till he removed it.

"B-b-bomb?" she croaked.

"Hold still. Looks homemade." His tone was sharper than he'd intended. He worked to untie the rope from her ankles.

Several frustrating minutes passed as he worked.

Libby whispered, "G-g-g—" She swallowed, then tried again. "G-get out."

"We will. We will." He leveled his gaze on her. "It's here, Libby. The DMBE is here. Todd dumped it in the well. He didn't know the aquifer flows southward. He didn't know the contamination would be flowing away from Crooked Arrow. He tried to kill you. And he meant to destroy the well and the evidence along with it."

Libby lay prone, her body battered from her ordeal. "H-he's c-c-crazy."

"Or he's as sane as you and me," Rafe said. "And he's trying to cover some very crazy behavior." Then he felt a flicker inside. "So you saw him? It was Todd who brought you here?"

She could only shake her head. "F-face covered."

"Don't talk. It's okay now." Disappointment walloped him. Well, the police would catch him. They had to. All that really mattered was that Libby was alive and safe. Or she soon would be.

The rope came loose, and Rafe smoothly set the dangerous-looking contraption by the hole.

"Come on," he told Libby, gathering her up in his arms. "We're leaving this one to the professionals. I'll tell the police to get the bomb squad out here to defuse that thing. I'm getting you out of here."

The night wind carried the faint sound of sirens. Libby was free, sitting in the cab of Rafe's truck. He'd just tucked his jacket around her shoulders and viciously bruised upper arms when a long row of police cars and an ambulance turned onto the well road, their lights flashing red.

"Sweetheart," he said softly, "things are going to get hectic in a minute. They're going to want to take you to the medical center. But I need to know…did you hear any of what I said in there?"

"H-heard you c-calling me."

He smoothed away a smudge of dirt high on her cheekbone. "I've been stubborn, honey. You were smarter than me all along. You recognized that this thing between us is special and that it's bigger than us. I was stupid to try to ignore it. I love you. And if you'll have me, I want to spend the rest of my life proving just how much."

In the moonlight, her vivid eyes expressed a coyness he'd never before seen. It was cute. And sexy as hell.

"D-didn't you also say something about being w-w-willful?"

He inhaled sharply, a half grin cocking his mouth to one side. "You did hear me."

She smiled and was evidently more relaxed now as her speech came smoother, easier.

Libby shrugged, pain causing her to flinch. "Well, yeah. B-but it might take a whole lifetime before I can g-get you to admit again that you've been both stubborn and willful. I just wanted to hear you say it now.'' She curled up against his chest. ''Now, r-repeat that last little bit.''

''What? That I was stupid to try—''

''No,'' she whispered. ''The very last bit.''

''The part where I said I love you?''

She smiled. And his heart took flight.

He covered her mouth with his, kissing her heatedly. His blood raged, his groin tightened. And Rafe knew the love he felt for Libby would burn bright through all eternity.

Life—and love—he'd discovered, were precious and beautiful gifts. Never again would he take either for granted. The woman in his arms was amazing. She'd suffered her own sorrow in the past, had been hurt and tossed aside. And when she'd offered Rafe her heart, he, too, wounded her with rejection. Yet here she was, willing to forget the pain of yesterday and focus only on the future. She was a wonder, someone who could teach him much through her willingness to forgive and forget, through her willingness to trust, her willingness to love.

''I love you, Rafe,'' she whispered against his mouth. ''My love. My Dark Wind.'' She pulled back. ''Just like Alex Featherstone said, darkness is like a protective blanket that shields. You've been my protector. And like the wind, you've blown love and contentment and happiness into my life.''

When he'd first revealed his Mokee-kittuun name to her, she had expressed that she thought it depressing. And until this moment, he, too, had thought so. However, his soul was no longer empty. It was filled to overflowing with the love he felt for Libby.

"Remember how I told you I was waiting for the sun to rise?" he softly asked.

She nodded.

He combed his fingers through her glorious hair. "Well, it's daybreak. And I've never seen a more beautiful dawn. Quick," he said in a rush, the sound of car doors slamming shut, men's shouts intruding in on them. "Before we're overrun with police and rescue workers...tell me you'll spend forever with me. Tell me you'll be my wife."

Her eyes glittered with happy tears. "Oh, Rafe. Yes!" And then she kissed him soundly.

* * * * *

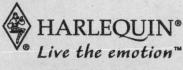

Three modern Gothic stories
about the legend of an 18th-century inn...

MYSTERIES *of* LOST ANGEL INN

Containing three editorially connected novellas.

USA TODAY
Bestselling Author

Evelyn
ROGERS

and

Kathleen
O'BRIEN

Debra
WEBB

Every twenty years—according to legend—someone will
die violently at the Lost Angel Inn. Two decades have passed
since the last death and three women have come to the inn.
Will one of them be the next victim?

Available in September 2004.

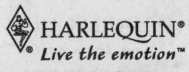

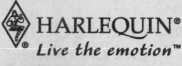